"We're not safe here."

Adam started the boat, then turned his attention to her. "What we have to figure out is who wants to kill you. That's it. I don't care why at this point. But odds are that the guy who came into the room and tried to smother you, who stabbed me, is the same man who tried to strangle you to death on the island. Who is it? Who is trying to kill you, Cobie? What does it have to do with the book we found?"

"I'm not sure. It's hard to stay focused on the details, to remember, when you're fighting for your life." Had her father trusted the wrong man? Someone who'd killed him?

And what if Adam had died all because of this treasure someone wanted? Cobie wasn't sure she could live with herself if that had happened. Nor was she sure she could keep her resentment and continue holding Adam responsible for Brad's death. The thought of losing him...well, that nearly undid her.

Shivering, Cobie wiped the mist out of her eyes. She had the sense that danger was circling her, closing in on her, and she didn't know if she would escape alive.

Elizabeth Goddard is an award-winning author of over twenty novels, including the romantic mystery *The Camera Never Lies*—winner of a prestigious Carol Award in 2011. After acquiring her computer science degree, she worked at a software firm before eventually retiring to raise her four children and become a professional writer. In addition to writing, she homeschools her children and serves with her husband in ministry.

Books by Elizabeth Goddard

Love Inspired Suspense

Mountain Cove

Buried
Untraceable
Backfire
Submerged

Freezing Point
Treacherous Skies
Riptide
Wilderness Peril

Visit the Author Profile page at Harlequin.com.

SUBMERGED

ELIZABETH GODDARD

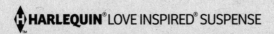
HARLEQUIN® LOVE INSPIRED® SUSPENSE

LOVE INSPIRED BOOKS

Recycling programs
for this product may
not exist in your area.

ISBN-13: 978-0-373-67710-8

Submerged

Copyright © 2015 by Elizabeth Goddard

www.Harlequin.com

Printed in U.S.A.

For as high as the heavens are above the earth,
so great is His love for those who fear Him;
as far as the east is from the west,
so far has He removed our transgressions from us.
—*Psalms* 103:12-13

There are so many unsung heroes in the world, and I want to dedicate this story, as well as the entire Mountain Cove series, to all the search-and-rescue volunteers, the everyday people who answer the call to save strangers. And more than that, I dedicate this story to my personal hero, my husband, who has sacrificed so that I could spend too many hours out of every day in a world far, far away from him.

Acknowledgments

Thank you to my many writing friends who've encouraged me along the way. I couldn't have remained on this writing journey, especially early on, without you. I so appreciate the assistance my new friends in Juneau, Alaska, have offered continually throughout the writing of this series. I know the accuracy and the details of southeast Alaska have made for a much better story. I'm grateful to my agent, Steve Laube, for making me feel as if I'm his only client on most days. And as always, I'm so thankful for my editor Elizabeth Mazer for believing in me and my stories.

ONE

Dread crept up Cobie MacBride's spine. She'd never wanted to do this again. But here she was, facing her past in an attempt to gain a future. Facing a cave again, when she never wanted to see the inside of another one after the caving accident that had taken her brother Brad's life. She was here today for an entirely different reason, and yet it was all connected.

She'd expected a yawning opening, but instead she stared at the slim crawlway into the cave, low and vertical. A muddy chute into the underworld. A trickle of water ran down the towering rock face; velvety moss covered the ground and entrance. Surrounded by the lush greenery of ferns, the cave—a product of this karst-laden land—had remained hidden on Kessler Island, one of thousands of islands, most uninhabited, in southeast Alaska's Tongass National Forest.

Her archaeologist father had found it and written about it in his journal. That was the only reason she was here. He had been missing for six months now and presumed dead. They'd been estranged for years, until last Christmas when he'd called and claimed he wanted to make up for the past and would be in touch soon.

She never heard from him again.

Peering at the cave now—a place where he'd recently been and walked, that one last connection to him—Cobie knew she wouldn't go inside alone. Bad enough she'd arrived on the island via floatplane ahead of Laura and Jen, two spelunking buddies she'd lost touch with over the years who had been eager enough to go on this venture with her. After she'd dumped her pack containing extra clothes, food and other supplies at the public-use cabin, she'd figured she could scout out one of the two cave entrances detailed in her father's journal. He'd made sure that someone delivered the journal into her hands, leaving her with more questions than answers. All she wanted to do was go inside and see the last thing her father had written about.

The whir of a boat in the distance pulled her thoughts back to the present. *That must be Laura and Jen now. Better head back to the cabin.*

She reached for her bottled water.

From behind, a strong arm wrapped around her throat in a choke hold and squeezed. Her air supply cut off, Cobie didn't have time to think, just react. She twisted and pulled and kicked, but the man's thick muscled arm didn't budge. She wasn't breaking free from this.

She wanted to ask him why he was trying to kill her. Persuade him to let her go. But she couldn't croak out the words. Pressure built in her head. Darkness edged her vision.

Cobie couldn't die like this. She was the only one of her family left. But what to do? Her life was slipping away…

He'd gripped her tightly enough that she couldn't head-butt. She'd never wrestle his arm away from her throat. She let go, flailing. Her lungs screamed. Her head felt as if it would explode.

God, please, help me!

Her hand bumped a rock. *A rock!* That was the only way. She had seconds before she passed out. Or before he crushed her throat completely.

Her fingers reached for the rock, grappling, feeling the rough edges, unable to secure it, until finally she gripped the weapon. Prickles of light flashed across her vision. Before she was gone, before it was too late, she put all her strength into slamming the rock into his head.

Immediately, his grip loosened. He dropped her and collapsed.

Cobie crashed to the ground, sharp pebbles and sticks cutting into her knees. She reached for her neck—had to be bruised—as she sucked in oxygen. Rolling to her side, she let her vision clear, the pressure from her head ease.

Someone had just tried to kill her. Worse, he was still there. She gathered her strength and pushed to her feet. Still wobbly, she pressed a hand against the gray wall of limestone towering above her. She eyed the man. He was clad in a gray rain jacket over a green plaid shirt, and she guessed he was above average height and weight. Strong. But she couldn't identify him, couldn't even tell the color of his hair. He wore a black knit ski mask to hide every feature that mattered. That made this attempted murder appear premeditated; he must have planned to kill someone today. Planned to kill her.

Blood oozed from the rip in his mask where she'd hit him, and she could see the gash at his temple. Cobie pressed her hands to her own head. Had she just killed a man? It was self-defense, but still it was too much to comprehend. Nausea surged in her stomach. Then she saw his chest rise and fall. So he wasn't dead. She stepped closer, unsure what to do now.

Pull his mask off? See who it was? Or should she try to put as much distance between them as she could before he woke up?

Cobie crept forward. If he remained unconscious, she could slip the mask off. Identify him to the police or whoever amounted to law on this forsaken island. He groaned. Lifted a hand to his forehead. Cobie froze. Held her breath.

If she could get closer she could knock him out again. Maybe. But if he woke up completely and she was still here, she was dead.

She took off into the forest. Had to get deep into the thick of it. She could make her way around to the cabin somehow. She had to warn her friends. There was no cell service out here, and her SAT phone was at the cabin. At least Laura always carried a weapon. She might have to use it. Cobie had been told there weren't bears on the island, so she hadn't worried about that kind of protection, but she hadn't considered there might be the two-legged kind of predator to worry about.

There shouldn't even be anyone else on this small island. Not until later in the day when other cavers were coming to map the cave for the forest service. That much she'd found out, at least, and she'd wanted to beat them to it. See the place the way her father had seen it. Now she was regretting that she'd ever come. And, worse, that she'd invited friends, possibly putting them in danger.

Why had he tried to kill her?

Cobie pressed through the thick forest, breathing hard, running as fast as she could. Hoping the man would forget about her. Consider her too much trouble to follow. Too much trouble to kill. Maybe he'd realize she wasn't the person he was after.

Behind her, leaves rustled. Limbs and sticks crashed. Like Bigfoot himself was tracking her.

Panic engulfed her. Coursed through her veins and left her timid and shaking. Afraid she wasn't going to survive this.

So many regrets.

Too many. *Oh, God, please give me another chance to set everything right. Please give me a chance to let go. I know I have to forgive.* So much bad had happened; she'd lost count of everything that she'd let sprout into bitterness and resentment.

Cobie pushed through the forest and stopped, leaning and flailing over the cliff's edge, a good forty feet above the waterline. She caught herself and stepped back. The sea cliff could be where the other entrance to the cave was, somewhere at the bottom.

Covering her mouth, she let out a sob and turned to face the forest behind her. A dark cloud had moved over the sun, turning the sky somber. Muting the lush green of the forest. Even the water of the strait, connecting with the ocean to the southwest, had turned black. Violent.

She was trapped.

She could hear him coming for her.

See the leaves moving.

He was getting closer.

Cobie turned to face the water surrounding the island. A boat. She saw a trawler. She waved and yelled and screamed, trying to draw the boat's attention. What did it matter if the man heard her calling for help? He was coming for her either way.

But the boat was too far away for anyone on board to hear her cries for help. Too far away to assist even if they did. Her knees buckled. She wanted to drop to the ground and beg for her life. But the killer wasn't interested in her words. Of that she was sure. If she stayed here, the man would kill her for reasons unknown. He didn't seem interested in giving or taking information from her.

Oh, God, I'm not ready to die. So much left to do yet. To figure out.

She couldn't stay where she was. But she could jump. And if she jumped, she just might miss the rocks. Then again, she could meet with a rocky death, but she wouldn't give him the satisfaction of killing her.

Still, a plunge into the water below gave her a better chance of a survival.

Cobie sent up one last prayer. She took a running, flying leap off the sea cliff.

Adam Warren's stomach churned as he leaned over the railing at the side of the trawler, struggling to get his sea legs. The waters of the strait to the southwest of Kessler Island had turned dark and rough as they flowed out of Chambers Passage, just one of the many waterways of the Inside Passage weaving through Alaska's panhandle.

He rubbed his eyes. Squinted. Was motion sickness making him hallucinate? What had he just seen? "Guys?"

"I saw her, too." Gary headed up the winding staircase to the bridge. Turned his parents' trawler to starboard.

Though far away, they'd been close enough to see what looked like long brown hair whipping around, jacket flying up to reveal a trim figure as she jumped into the crashing waves.

Everyone rushed to the bridge with Gary, the highest point on the boat. "What do you think? Suicide?"

Nate and Jared, two of Adam's caving buddies, scanned the depths with Adam as the trawler sliced through the rough waves.

"No." A sense of urgency wrapped around Adam. *Please, God, let her be okay.*

He quickly shrugged out of his rain jacket, preparing to dive in after her, if needed. But where was she? He grabbed the life buoy and prepared to toss it out. But depending on how she hit the water, at that height, she could have a compressed spine, or any number of other injuries. She'd drown if they didn't find her, if she wasn't already sinking from cold water shock response.

Then Nate sucked in a breath. "I see her! There she is!" He pointed at the water, miles and miles of water.

Gary steered the boat toward where Nate pointed.

Adam searched the waters, too. A head bobbed. She waved. But then she went under again. "Get this thing closer, will you?"

He couldn't swim faster than the trawler, so he'd have to bide his time. But if they didn't make it soon, she was going under for good. Gary was experienced enough at handling the boat. Adam trusted him to do his best, but it was still taking too long. Adam and his siblings volunteered on the North Face Mountain Search and Rescue Team—it gnawed at him to stand back and wait when someone needed help.

They neared the last place they saw the jumper, and Adam bounded down the steps to the lower deck and tossed the lifesaving buoy into the water. But the woman didn't surface again. Without hesitation he dived into the cold depths of the strait, then swam toward the ring he'd tossed.

He guessed the water temperature to be in the low fifties, maybe high forties. Brutal enough to send a person into cold incapacitation—the loss of control of hands and the muscles in the arms and legs. Before long, they would quit working altogether.

The water's usual dark blue was almost an inky

black, but as he dived beneath the surface it was crystal clear, so that he could see.

There.

He saw her well enough. She still had some fight in her, but her eyes were wide with terror as she fought a losing battle to the surface. Her limbs had become too cold and numb to make a difference. Soon Adam would also succumb. But she'd been in the water much longer than he had. He could do this. He could save her.

Had to save her. He couldn't fail again. Couldn't let someone drown again, though his best friend's death would always be on his head.

His lungs burned as he thrust toward her, seized her arm and, with all his strength, swam them to the surface. He grabbed the life buoy and pulled her out of the bitingly cold water. Nate and Jared tugged them toward the boat, and Adam held on to the woman. Water poured from her mouth as she coughed and choked.

Fueled by adrenaline, even his relief that she hadn't drowned couldn't slow his racing pulse. His buddies assisted them onto the trawler, and then forgot about Adam and ushered her inside the galley, where it was warm. Dripping and cold, Adam followed and saw Jared wrap a blanket around her. Her lips were blue in her pale face as she shivered and sat in the booth, still gasping for breath.

"You need to remain still. Get warmed up," Jared told them.

Adam knew Jared referred to post-rescue collapse. They had to wait until their systems had warmed up completely so their hearts would stabilize.

Before he slid into the booth beside her, she lifted the biggest bluest eyes he'd ever seen to meet his gaze.

Adam knew those eyes.

Stunned, he took a step back. She appeared equally surprised to see him. Maybe in the urgency of the rescue, recognition hadn't kicked in for either of them.

When Jared handed over a mug of microwaved cocoa, she eagerly took it. Adam wrapped his hand around the mug offered him, and settled in next to Cobie MacBride.

At one time, Cobie had been the only woman for him. She'd cured him of ever wanting to go through that again. Weird to think she didn't even know about the feelings he'd had.

"Thank you for saving me." She shook her head, stared into her cup. Her beautiful eyes had lost none of their grief from the tragedy that had left her brother dead, but some sort of wild terror swam in them now, as well.

"What happened?" Adam asked. "Why'd you jump?"

He wasn't sure he wanted to know the answer. He couldn't stand it if she said she'd been trying to kill herself. But he wouldn't believe it, either. She'd waved for them; she'd wanted their help. And if they hadn't been there? Adam clamped down on those thoughts.

"I didn't have a choice."

TWO

Was this some sort of dream? Nightmare?

The past few minutes washed over her. She struggled to grasp what had happened. The men stared at her, confusion on their faces. Bewildered herself, she frowned. How did she explain without sounding…well…crazy?

"What do you mean, you didn't have a choice?" Raw concern flashed in Adam's eyes.

That surprised her.

It had been so long since she'd seen him, been this close to him, old feelings tumbled over every other thought. She'd missed him. Shaking off the tangle of emotions, she hung her head and sighed.

"I need a minute to think." Gather her thoughts.

Almost equally as shocking as the events of the past few moments was the fact that Adam sat next to her, wrapped in his own wool blanket. He angled to look at her, his solid form a comforting presence compared with moments ago when another man had tried to kill her.

And if she was drawing comfort from his nearness, then that just proved how befuddled and exhausted she was. He'd pulled her from the depths, saved her life. She knew that. But it didn't make up for the past.

Adding to her anxiety, tumultuous waves rocked the trawler, much like the turmoil that tossed her mind. She tugged the blanket closer, tighter.

Adam was here with Jared, Nate and Gary, his long-time caving buddies. They'd been Brad's friends, as well.

Jared stepped from below deck into the small galley and lobbed them each a shirt and jeans. "Found some dry things."

Cobie stared at the clothes. Too big. She looked up at Jared.

He shrugged. "Adam is the smallest. You'll have to wear his clothes."

Adam slid from the booth and stood. "What's going on, Cobie?"

After that first punch-in-the-gut glance into Adam's face, Cobie hadn't wanted to look at him again. Hadn't she been thinking about him—how she needed to forgive—right before she jumped? God had some sense of humor. She lifted her gaze to meet his multicolored eyes. She'd never been able to decide if they were blue or green the way they seemed to change. All the hours she'd spent thinking about his eyes. But that was ancient history.

Finally Cobie caught her breath. Found her words.

"We need to call the police. Someone tried to kill me." Cobie pressed her face into her hands. "And Laura and Jen are on their way to the island. They should be there any minute. We'd planned to meet at the cabin to go caving. They were running late, so I went to the cave to scout it out. If they arrive and go looking for me, they could run right into the man who tried to kill me."

"What?" the male voices asked in unison.

She dropped her hands and stared at them, forcing urgency into her voice. "A man tried to strangle me. I ran away. I got trapped when he followed. I had no choice. I had to face him or jump."

Adam's strong jaw dropped along with the blanket. "Call 9-1-1."

"Coast Guard's all there is out here." Nate held up his cell. "And these don't work here at all."

"Then call the Coast Guard," she said. "Someone in authority needs to know."

Adam scraped the SAT phone from the counter. "I could call Ray. I told him we were mapping the cave and he said he might try to get some time off and join us."

"Ray?" Cobie asked.

"Forest Service Law Enforcement and Investigation. He's an agent. Investigates crimes. Drugs. Poaching. Anything illegal that happens out here."

Had she really almost been a victim? And now she would have to give a statement. Answer questions. Cobie's mind ran back over what had happened. Concern for her friends made her tense. If only she hadn't been such an idiot. The number where she could reach Laura was with the phone at the cabin.

Adam kept his gaze on her. "He's probably close. We'll ask him what to do. Tell him what happened."

Shivering, Cobie slipped out of the booth. "Can we go ahead and make our way to the other side of the island? Maybe we can intercept Laura and Jen. In the meantime, I'm changing into dry clothes."

"Why didn't you travel with your friends?" Jared leaned against the counter. "Why come alone?"

Adam cocked a brow.

"I took a seaplane. The pilot passes over these parts delivering mail and packages and people. My friends are coming by boat from the opposite direction. They were delayed, and I couldn't change my flight."

"Why not wait for them to arrive before exploring the cave?" Adam asked. "Why go alone?"

She was a big girl, but saying so would make it sound otherwise. "It shouldn't have been dangerous. There shouldn't have been someone else there—much less a man who wanted to kill me. Besides, he could have found me alone at the cabin, too."

Not wanting to say more, or hear a lecture, Cobie scuttled down the small stairway below deck. She didn't have to explain her actions to them. Adam said something to his friends, but she couldn't make out his words, then he followed her down.

"I'll show you where to go."

The quarters were tight. Hard to get lost on a boat this size. She could find her own way without his help, but she kept her thoughts to herself. He showed her the master cabin with its walk-around queen bed and then took her through the private guest cabin. Beyond that, berth to port, was a large guest room. Then to starboard, Adam showed her the shower with the private door back to the master cabin where they'd started. The former fishing boat had been refurbished into a near-luxurious recreational boat.

Clinging to the clothes she meant to change into, probably getting them wet as she did, Cobie hung back, near the door to the master cabin. "I thought you were calling your forest service friend."

"Jared is calling so I can change clothes, too. Gary will contact the Coast Guard. He's heading to the lagoon where your friends will probably anchor." The small space forced their proximity, and Adam stared down at her. "I... I'm glad you're okay, Cobie." He scraped his hand through his wet hair and looked away, then back at her. "It's good to see you."

She didn't miss the pain in his eyes.

"Thanks...thanks for saving me today." She wanted to tell him that it was good to see him, too, but she couldn't find the words. She'd never wanted to see him again.

His clothes were still wet, like hers, and must be cold, but there was a heat emanating from him. The way he looked at her now made that heat wrap around her. She didn't want to feel that from him, even though she was chilled to her bones.

He cleared his throat. "You can use this room to change."

"Okay, thanks." Cobie waited for him to leave.

He lifted a hand. Scratched the back of his head as if he was unsure what else to say. As if he wanted to say more.

Cobie knew she had more to say, too, and to a man she'd never wanted to see or speak to again. Could the day get any stranger? "I'll be right out."

He nodded. "Don't worry, Cobie. We'll find your friends and warn them."

"I hope so." Once she slipped inside and shut the door behind her, she quickly changed into the dry clothes she carried, though they'd grown damp from her clinging. They smelled like Adam. Musky and masculine and outdoorsy. The smells made more images rush back at her.

She pressed her face into the blue-and-gray-plaid sleeve and breathed in the scent. Made her dizzy. Memories of how she used to feel about the guy surged. But that's all those feelings were now. Memories.

Weird that he'd never even known.

Tears threatened behind her eyes. She dropped onto the bed to gather her composure before she faced Adam again.

She let her thoughts turn to the way he had looked at her. He seemed different somehow. Changed by that day as much as she had been. Especially five years later. Weird how a tragedy, added to a few years of separation, could change a person. And yet even though Adam was different now, plenty about him remained the same. He was…well…he could have been the next all-American hero to star in a Marvel movie, with those broad shoulders and lean, muscular biceps. And he was handsome enough to make plenty of girls swoon. But not Cobie. Not anymore.

At least that's what she tried to convince herself of, but it wasn't working because being next to Adam made her float like it had before Brad's death.

Cobie shoved herself to her feet. She was grateful that Adam had saved her today. Grateful for the spare too-big shirt and pants she wore now. But in spite of the few good memories that taunted her, she could never forget that Adam was to blame for her brother's death.

Adam stumbled around in the guest cabin, trying desperately to clear his thoughts. Cobie was here on this boat.

And someone had tried to kill her.

Thank You, Lord, for saving her.

Adam reminded himself that while he'd pulled her from the water, God had been the one to save her. Bittersweet, considering Adam hadn't been able to pull her brother from the water that day. Some things in life he'd never understand. He grabbed a towel and dried his hair. Pulled in a few calming breaths.

It took a lot for Adam to be in the same room with Cobie. He hadn't realized just how much. Funny how five years hadn't diminished how she affected him. At one time, she'd been the girl of his dreams. Now she was the girl he could never have. Even if he *could* have her, he couldn't want her or anyone. But none of that mattered. All that mattered was that he'd make sure she was safe.

He sucked in another breath. Opened the door.

Heading back to join the rest, he passed the master cabin. Was she still inside? Maybe he'd wait for her. He had a few questions before she talked to the authorities. Leaning against the wall, he noticed the boat rocked less. Gary must have made it to smoother waters.

The door whipped open.

Cobie's eyes widened. "You waited on me?"

"Yep." Feeling like an idiot, he shoved his hands in his pockets. He looked her up and down. She wore his clothes now. His shirt hung off her—jeans, too. He wouldn't be able to wear those again without thinking of her.

Reacting to his scrutiny, she looked down, held out her arms. "What? You don't like my new duds?"

Adam smiled. Good she could find some humor. It made things bearable.

"How are you doing?" He had to go and shoot down her smile.

Her brows scrunched. "How do you think?"

His pulse jumped when he caught sight of her throat. Adam reached over and tipped her chin up. At the bruise on her neck, anger boiled in his gut. He seriously wanted to hurt the man who did this to her. Glancing at her eyes, he saw everything inside her laid bare.

Then she was in his arms. He wasn't sure how—if he'd made the move or she had—but she was in them. And he held her tight. He couldn't lose her, too. He'd lost his best friend, her brother.

God, I can't lose her, too.

She didn't sob into his shirt. Not like the day Brad had died. But he thought maybe she wanted to. Maybe *he* wanted to sob over all that had happened to keep them apart. Over his role in Brad's death. And over what had happened to her today.

"Cobie," he whispered into her soft, still wet hair. How long had he wanted to tangle his fingers in that thick mane?

She stiffened.

Cobie stepped away from him. *That's right. Keep up that wall.* That would keep them both in line. He couldn't believe he'd slipped. Let himself think about how she felt in his arms for even a second.

"Why would someone try to kill you?" he asked.

"You think I know?" She shoved by him.

That had been the wrong thing to say. But how could he get answers without questions? He followed her into the galley, where Jared and Nate both looked up.

"Ray called back after I left a message," Jared said. "I told him everything."

"What'd he say?" Adam smelled coffee brewing. He was glad someone had thought to put some on.

"He's on his way. Will meet us near the beach."

"How long?"

"An hour, maybe more."

"He asked if Cobie was injured." Nate studied Cobie. "If you needed medical attention. I told him I thought you were okay for now. Was I wrong?"

She shrugged. "I'll be good when I know Laura and Jen are safe."

Adam shared a look with Nate. She needed to have a doctor check her out all the same, with her throat bruised that way.

"We'll do our best, Cobie." Jared poured her coffee and handed her a steaming mug.

Adam left Cobie in good hands. She didn't want to see him anyway. He made his way to the outside bridge up top where Gary steered the trawler. Since there was a steering station inside, he could have stayed in the galley with the rest of them where it was nice and warm, but Gary preferred to experience the full effect of being on the water. Wanted to feel the weather and smell the ocean. And maybe Gary wanted to step away from the drama they'd all just endured, Cobie most especially.

The island, one of many in southeast Alaska, loomed large ahead of them—steep bedrock and limestone exposures looked as though they'd been pushed up and out of the ocean by something ancient. The view of the greenery topping the rock of an island made Adam's breath catch. Also made him second-guess his decision to explore the world outside the panhandle of Alaska—to get away from Mountain Cove and all the reminders of his failures. Since his business had burned down not two months ago he had this chance, this one chance, to do something different with his life.

But the beauty of the region tugged at him now, tightening the grip on his heart.

With the rain and fog and mist, lakes and rivers everywhere, fjords and glaciers, what more could he want? What more did a man need? Except Adam wanted and needed something he couldn't put his finger on. After this expedition to map a cave, he already had the next three months planned out, and he wouldn't be spending them in Alaska.

His sister, Heidi, had extracted one promise from him—be home by Christmas. As if it mattered if he was there or not. She and his brothers had lives of their own now. Families of their own. Adam was the odd man out. He wasn't sure they would miss him if he didn't show for Christmas. But he hadn't even left yet and he was at a crossroad. Cobie suddenly turning up in his life again made for more indecision.

Yep. A serious fork in a road he had yet to travel.

"Looks like we're almost there," Adam said.

"There's another boat anchored near the shore." Gary gestured. "See? Just through there. Could be Cobie's friends."

"I hope they're not already on the island," Adam said. "They need to be warned about Cobie's attacker. Did you see any other boats coming or going?"

"No." Gary eyed Adam. "He must have left before we got here."

"Or…he's still on the island."

THREE

"That's Laura's boat." Concern for her friends kept Cobie on edge. "We're wasting time standing here."

She tugged the hood of the too-big rain jacket she'd pulled over her head. She'd put on Adam's extra pair of rain pants, too, over her borrowed clothes. Although she wore gear meant to keep out the pouring rain, she knew that eventually it would find its way in and under the protective clothing. This was a temperate rain forest, after all. Wearing rain gear was an exercise in futility.

Nate and Jared stood on one side of her, Adam on the other.

Water dripped off his hood as his blue-green eyes turned dark, watching her. "Looks empty."

"They're probably both on the island looking for me. We have to warn them."

"Ray said to stay put," Jared said. "Wait until he got here."

"We *can't* wait. My friends are in danger. We have to save them."

"You know she's right." Adam climbed into the skiff they'd towed that would take them where the trawler couldn't go.

He pulled a weapon out of a holster and checked it. Chills ran down Cobie's spine. She was leading Adam and his friends into a potentially deadly situation, but she didn't have a clue what else to do.

His jaw set, Adam looked up at Cobie. "You're not going."

"What are you talking about?" Panic and rage boiled inside. "I'm going. You can't keep me here. I'll swim if I have to. What difference does it make if I get wet? I'm wet already."

At the thought of getting into that water again, a knot swelled in her throat. Adam had to know it was an idle threat on her part, which made it worthless. Ignoring Cobie, Jared and Nate climbed into the skiff. There was no room for her; it was that small. Now she was spitting mad, but that wouldn't help her make her case. She pushed her frustration down.

"Look, I have to be with you. Laura and Jen are going to freak out when they see you. They're going to be worried about me if I'm not at the cabin. They're going to think you're the bad guys." *Maybe.* She wasn't sure what they would think. If they had only just arrived on the island, they were probably still looking for Cobie without realizing anything was wrong. It was worth a shot to convince Adam to let her go along.

Jared climbed out. "She's right, Adam."

Cobie quickly climbed in before Jared could change his mind, giving him a quick squeeze on his arm and a thank-you. Adam's jaw tensed. He didn't look happy, but that wasn't her problem. He grabbed the oars and rowed the boat to shore.

They made it to the small sandy beach, the only place they could easily get ashore, away from the rocks and coral reefs that surrounded the rest of the island. She'd been fortunate to survive her jump off the bluff.

Thank You, Lord. She'd taken a leap of faith, as it were, knowing she'd either sink or swim. She'd sunk all right.

And Adam had pulled her from certain death.

Cobie shrugged off the memory and helped Adam and Nate secure the boat.

"How do we get to the cabin?" Adam's rigid tone set her on edge, but she knew that deep down he was only worried about her. She wondered if he'd finally learned to think about consequences—something he'd never bothered to do in the past. He'd been reckless with her brother's life, after all.

She pointed. "It's just there. The trail is over-grown. Not many people come here, but enough do, I guess."

Her father had. Others before him, too. Hard to believe the cave was mostly unexplored. Uncharted and undiscovered. There were hundreds of caves in southeast Alaska that they knew of. Many more they didn't. And plenty had yet to be explored or mapped.

Cobie trekked behind Adam and Nate up the barely visible trail that would take them to the cabin. The same trail she'd taken earlier when the pilot had dropped her off. He'd escorted her to the cabin. When he'd expressed concern about leaving her alone, she had assured him her friends would arrive soon. He had a schedule to keep and had to leave, but he promised to stop by after his deliveries to check on her. Billy seemed like a nice enough guy, and she knew people who knew him in Mountain Cove. She could trust him.

As they climbed higher, the Sitka spruce grew thicker, and the birds chirped. In the distance, sea lions barked. Cobie's encounter with the man bent on killing her seemed surreal. To think, a couple of hours ago this island had been a peaceful refuge. Now her fear gauge inched upward by the minute. What if the man was still on the island? What if he'd hurt Laura and Jen? What if he hurt Adam and his friends because Cobie had gotten them involved?

"Shouldn't we call out for them?" Cobie glanced up, searched the trees above. Small animals scuttled across the branches. "They could be anywhere on the island."

They could be in trouble.

"True enough, but until we know what we're up

against, I'd prefer to take the stealth approach." As soon as he'd said the words, Adam stopped.

Nate did the same behind him, as did Cobie.

"I can see the cabin up ahead in the clearing," Adam said.

"Let's go." She tried to hurry past him.

He held his arm out, clutching her waist, holding her back. "We don't know if it's safe."

"Then you'd better be prepared to use that weapon." Cobie shrugged free and ran toward the cabin. "Laura! Jen!"

Adam held back a few choice words. But what he'd said to Cobie came back to bite him.

We don't know if it's safe.

Those were the same exact words Brad had said to him when he'd tried to persuade his best friend to go down deeper into the cave they were exploring. Adam hadn't heeded Brad then, and Brad had been the one to die. Life certainly wasn't fair. Didn't pick the person who deserved to live over the person who deserved to die.

The guilt was crushing, except Cobie wouldn't give him a chance to stop and catch his breath. Gather his thoughts. That was the only good going on here. He rushed after her, but she was already out in the open, out of the protective cover of the trees, and yelling at the top of her lungs. Whoever was in the cabin had to know they had company by now.

With his gun in hand, he readied himself to defend them if it came to that.

"Cobie, wait!"

Adam caught up to her, grabbed her arm, pulled her back behind him. "At least let me go first. Let me protect you."

Cobie opened her mouth to argue when the door to the cabin opened. Adam's heart jumped to his throat. He threw himself in front of Cobie.

A tall brunette stepped out of the cabin and pointed her weapon at Adam. "Let her go."

"Laura! Wait. This is my friend Adam." Cobie stepped out from behind Adam.

Laura frowned and lowered her weapon. "I thought…"

Cobie ran to Laura. They hugged. Another woman, dirty-blond hair, short and sturdy like an athlete, joined the hug fest. Adam stood in the rain watching, the rapid beat of his heart keeping time with the drops. He dragged in a few breaths. That had been too close. Two friends trying to protect a mutual friend had nearly gotten one of them killed.

"Come inside." Cobie and Laura pulled Adam and Nate into the cabin.

Cobie made the introductions. Laura cocked a brow when she recognized either Adam or his name—he wasn't sure. He might have seen her with Cobie years ago, now that he thought about it. But she'd changed something. Lost weight. Dyed her hair. And the other woman, Jen, didn't look happy to see him.

"We thought something had happened to you," Jen said. "We went to the cave looking for you. You didn't tell me you were bringing other friends, Cobie. Guy friends."

"No, wait. You don't understand." Cobie started to explain but then stopped. "What's…what's all this?"

Laura and Jen moved out of Adam's line of sight so he could see gear was strewn across the floor. Bags ripped. Junk tossed.

"I don't know. We found it like this. And you were gone." Laura flashed a suspicious look at Adam. "That's why we were so worried."

Cobie covered her mouth and glanced at Adam. Her eyes said everything she couldn't say. This guy had tried to kill her. Had rummaged through her things. Why? Adam wanted to hug her to him. He thought about that brief moment on the trawler when she'd been in his arms. He wanted to comfort her like that again. Protect her. But he wasn't the man for that.

"What's going on, Cobie?" Laura asked, looking from Adam to Cobie. Nate didn't merit a glance.

Cobie told them about the man who had tried to strangle her to death at the cave. About the jump off the bluff. And about how she'd almost drowned before Adam pulled her out.

Jen leaned against the wall and slid down. "Gotta sit down. My legs are shaking."

"Mine, too." Cobie joined her on the floor. Laura was next.

Tears welled in all three women's eyes. Adam looked away. He couldn't take watching them cry. It wasn't that he had a hard heart. No. It was the exact opposite. He was too softhearted for his own good, and that had always gotten him into trouble. He had to work hard to protect himself. At least Cobie's friends were here to comfort her. Adam wanted to join them in their efforts, but he couldn't afford to let his heart grow soft again when it came to Cobie.

Nate shifted around the cabin, drawing Adam's attention. He moved closer to his friend, away from the women who huddled next to Cobie, talking among themselves.

"The guy could still be here," Nate said under his breath. "We need to keep our guard up."

"Yep. Wish Ray would get here."

Adam looked around at Cobie's things all over the floor. Man, she'd brought a lot of stuff. How long had she been planning to stay? But then she'd need fresh clothing after she explored the cave, and maybe after she stepped outside, too. This could have gotten awkward real fast, considering he and his friends had planned to use this cabin while they mapped the cave. Had Cobie made a reservation, too? Or had someone overbooked the cabin?

"Cobie, you missing anything?"

"I don't know. What could I have that anyone would want?"

Someone knocked on the door. The women against the wall yelped. Laura stood, pressed her hand against her gun. Adam frowned. "You might be good with your weapon, but I don't need you shooting a hole in my friend."

She scowled. "How do you know it's him?"

"Is Cobie's attacker going to knock?"

"Stranger things have happened." Jen was on her feet, pulling Cobie up with her.

Adam's gut churned. What if? He pressed his hand against the sidearm in his shoulder holster. Approached the door.

"Nate? Adam? You in there? It's Ray."

Relief flooded Adam and he opened the door to his stern-faced friend.

"I told you to stay put."

Adam shrugged and swung the door wider. "Might as well come in."

Ray stepped inside the cabin followed by another shorter man, about ten years older—probably the friend Ray had mentioned he'd invited to explore the cave. "Ladies, this is Ray Hamburg," Adam said. "He's a special agent with the Law Enforcement and Investigation division of the Forest Service."

Ray didn't give Adam his usual warm grin; he kept his authoritative expression in place. He'd been a park ranger before moving over to LEI. Maybe he would solve this quickly. "And this is Mel Timbrook. Also LEI. Looks like we have an investigation to get behind us. I headed off the Coast Guard. We're usually not the first to respond, but I'm already here and this is my region."

Mel and Ray looked around the room. Then Ray spoke again. "Looks like the cave-mapping expedition has turned into something much different. Someone want to tell me what's going on?"

Face pale, Cobie stepped forward. "I... Someone tried to kill me."

Adam didn't miss Ray's attention on Cobie's neck or the anger that he worked to suppress as she told him how a man had tried to strangle her to death. Adam experienced the same rage after the initial shock of pulling Cobie from the water. That someone could do that to anyone. That someone could do that to Cobie MacBride.

Her voice shook as she relayed the facts, and Adam relived every terrifying detail with her. He remembered the moment when he'd seen someone jump from the bluff. The image of her underneath the water before he was able to grab her—her face pale, the terror of certain death in her eyes. And that moment when he realized the jumper was Cobie hit him like a blunt object.

The big adventure he'd planned away from Alaska over the next few months had been an attempt to escape the past he shared with this woman. Instead he was getting sucked right back in. But he had to keep her safe. Find this guy before he succeeded in killing her.

How could he protect Cobie? How could he be part of her life again and get his life back at the same time? Because there was no way he wanted to get wrapped up in her world again. If he had to, in order to protect her, in order to find this guy, then how could he possibly protect his heart?

FOUR

She thought Ray's questions would never end.

Cobie leaned against the wall on the far side of the small log cabin as though that would give them privacy. Mel hung back and listened. Outside, the wind gusted, bringing more rain and blowing the wet weather through the island. Though a couple of portable lamps burned in the corners, the cabin grew darker with the storm. Nate started a fire in the fireplace that sent shadows dancing along the walls. She'd taken off her rain gear and, though she was still layered in Adam's flannel shirt over a T-shirt, she grew chilled, in body and spirit.

To his credit, Ray was attentive and concerned while he took notes, never showing any skepticism, although the story Cobie told sounded implausible, even to her own ears. Still, Adam and his friends had seen her jump. And her neck revealed evidence that someone had assaulted her. Had the villain stood at the top of the bluff and looked down just to make sure she didn't resurface? She certainly hadn't looked back to check, and Adam and his friends had been focused on her. Did her would-be killer know she was still alive?

Ray flipped to a new page in his notebook. "Tell me again why you'd come alone?"

She fought the need to roll her eyes. "My friends were on their way. Would have been here within the hour. I didn't see the harm in going by the cave first to get the lay of the land. It shouldn't have been dangerous. There's not supposed to be anyone else on this island."

"Normally that's true enough, and I haven't seen any DTO activity in this area, either."

"DTO?"

"Drug traffic organization."

Cobie hugged herself tighter. "Maybe...maybe they're hiding drugs in the cave and didn't want anyone to find it? Could be that's why the man tried to kill me."

Ray studied her, considering her words. "We'll find out soon enough." He reviewed his notes. "You said you knew about the cavers planning to map the cave, and you wanted to go in ahead of them. Why?"

"The truth is I wanted the cave to myself, and my friends wouldn't distract me as much as another group might. They might prevent us or interfere with our plans."

Ray's manner was easygoing and so far he'd kept

his face unreadable, but Cobie caught suspicion in the angle of his head. "How so?"

"What does it matter? What does any of this have to do with the man who tried to kill me?" His question made her feel as if she'd been the one to commit a crime, but she didn't dare say that. That would give him ammunition to ask more questions about why she was getting defensive. Or if she had committed a crime, which she hadn't.

"Humor me. Maybe it has nothing at all to do with your attacker, but I'm digging, asking questions hoping that I'll get at why someone tried to kill you today. Okay?" His smile disarmed her.

"Okay."

The man was good at what he did, no doubt there. "Did anyone else know you were coming here today?" Ray continued.

The back of her throat grew tight. "No, there is no one else. I'm a dentist, and my office staff knew I was heading to an island, but Laura and Jen were the only ones who knew which island."

"Any particular reason you chose this island and cave?" Ray blinked up at her.

Again, why did her reasons matter? But she wouldn't antagonize a man trying to help her resolve this. "I… My father wrote about this cave in his journal. It was the last entry—the most recent. I haven't seen him in years. I thought… I wanted to see something he'd seen. Walk where he'd walked.

I know it sounds crazy, but I thought I could get some closure."

Ray had been writing in his notebook again, but he lifted his gaze and studied Cobie. "Closure?"

"He disappeared six months ago."

Someone behind her gasped. Adam stepped forward. "Cobie, I'm sorry. I had no idea."

"It's… He was absent in my life long before he went missing." She shrugged, trying for an indifference she didn't feel. She hadn't wanted it to mean so much. But she was at this cave for that reason. Her mother had died when she was born, and her father and brother were all she had. Except her father had barely been part of her life or Brad's life because his occupation required travel. He was even more distant, if possible, after Brad's death. Then last Christmas, he'd called like always, but this time he'd told her he wanted to make up for lost time. To make up for the past. He just had something to take care of first. And those last words kept Cobie from believing that anything would ever change. There was always something more important than family in her father's life.

But her indifferent words to Ray had done damage. Something behind his eyes changed. Next to her, Adam shifted on his feet. Cobie fought to keep her composure. She didn't need complete strangers seeing her pain. Didn't want Adam to see it, either.

Flipping his notebook closed, Ray gestured behind Cobie. "You and your friends can wait here, or we can escort you to your boat to wait there while we search the island. It might take a while. We'll look for your attacker, though I doubt he's still here. We'll gather evidence if we find any."

That he hadn't asked her more questions, especially at the news of her father's disappearance, surprised her.

"Are you saying we can get into the cave today?" Nate asked.

"I can't say for sure now, but I'll know more in a couple of hours. I had planned to explore the cave with you, and we'll do that together, after we decide it's safe."

"You don't think he could be hiding in the cave?" Laura spoke up.

"That remains to be seen. But if he has any sense, he's long gone," Ray said. "What'll it be? Stay here or go to the boats?"

"We could chow down back on the boat. I'm getting hungry," Nate said. "Besides, Gary will want to know what's happening."

"Okay, that settles it," Mel said. "Everyone back to the boats. We'll escort you there."

"Should we leave our things, then?" Cobie asked.

"I don't think anyone else is going to bother your stuff. Plus, after we search the island, I might want to look at the damage done here again. Is that okay with you?"

"Sure."

Adam stepped up to speak to her, misery apparent in his eyes. But Laura and Jen got in his way, intentionally or accidentally blocking him; Cobie wasn't sure. She snatched up a few of her own clothes from her bag—eager to wear something that fit, eager to be free of Adam's clothes, though she slipped back into his rain jacket. And then her friends ushered her out like bodyguards. Ray and Mel followed them to the beach.

Laura led the way and climbed into an inflatable dinghy, Jen behind her. Ray approached Cobie before she got into the dinghy. "We're going to look for evidence of another boat on the beach, though that alone won't prove anything. Then we'll head up to the cave entrance where you say the attack happened. If we can find the specific rock you hit him with, we may at least get DNA evidence."

Adam joined them. "What about Cobie, Ray? She's not safe."

Ray tucked his chin. "He's right. Until we know more, you need to be aware of your surroundings."

"That's it?" Adam clenched his fists. "Just be aware of her surroundings? She needs protection."

"And she has it," Laura said, brandishing her weapon.

"Cobie, you and your friends should go home." Adam pressed his hand on her shoulder. "This isn't a place you should stay, with this creep still out there. He knows you're here. He could come back and try again."

"I came here to get answers, Adam. I'm not leaving without them."

The rain had finally stopped.

Adam stood at the stern of Laura's boat. He needed to speak to Cobie. When he opened the hatch to head down the steps below deck, feminine voices rose to meet him. The tone was serious. He tried to make enough noise so they'd know he was on his way down. He didn't want to hear anything he shouldn't. Cobie's friends didn't like him; of that, he was sure.

She had her reasons for being at odds with him, but in spite of that, there was some sort of crazy electricity that sparked between them every time he saw her. Did she feel it, too? Even if she did, what did it matter? After what had happened, Adam would never let himself be hurt like that again. Secretly loving his best friend's sister from a distance, watching the pain he'd caused, had scarred him. His actions, his poor judgment, had cost a life, changed lives and caused his own pain, forever affecting them all.

The thoughts weighed heavily on him, but he shook them off. He had more important matters to focus on. He paused before taking the steps down.

"I wish we didn't have to head back tomorrow,"

Laura said. "I'm sorry I couldn't spend more time with you."

"That's why we need to do this today. See the cave if the powers that be will allow us inside. We'll join Adam and his group if we have to."

"I'm proud of you. I know these last few years have been hard. Having Adam here makes it worse, I'm sure."

Adam cringed. Why hadn't they heard him? Why had he stopped and listened? Now he figured he should turn around and go back to the boat that housed people who liked him. His friends. But he would finish what he started. He clomped down the steps and into the galley, making his presence known. No turning back now.

The three women stared wide-eyed at him.

"Uh, sorry. Thought you'd hear me coming down. Didn't mean to surprise you." For that matter, Adam could have been Cobie's attacker and he would have caught them all off guard. So much for the overprotective, gun-brandishing Laura.

Tension crackled in the cabin.

"Are you hungry?" Jen grabbed a plate. "Might as well eat while we wait to get back on the island. I made my special—macaroni and cheese."

Adam pulled off his hood and ran a hand through his tangled hair, his gaze snagging on Cobie's amazing blue eyes. But she averted them. "No, thanks. I've already eaten. I...came to see Cobie."

"Well, here she is. You see her." Laura stirred the macaroni and cheese on her plate as if she was angry with it.

They weren't making it easy for him. He saw the hint of a smile on Cobie's pretty lips. She thought this was funny. When she dared to glance at him, he caught her gaze and trapped it with his own. She didn't look away this time.

"I need to talk to you when you're done eating."

"You can talk to me now."

He hesitated, glancing at her friends. "All right. Mind if I sit down?"

"Make yourself at home," Laura said.

Adam shrugged out of his extra raincoat. Hung it on the rack. He took the chair across from Cobie. "Nothing from Ray yet. Maybe they caught the guy. But he should contact us soon."

Cobie looked down at her plate. Shoved the cheesy pasta around. Either Jen's special wasn't so special, or his appearance had ruined their appetites.

Adam measured his words. He'd never felt more unsure of himself. He used to be confident, even overconfident. So much had changed. Years did that to people. Years and tragedies.

"Back in the cabin. When you talked to Ray—"

"What's really bothering you?" she asked.

Her tone begged him to get on with it. So be it.

"I'm sorry about your father, Cobie. I had no idea he's missing."

Cobie kept her gaze on the table. The other two stared at him as if they wished he would go away. Get out of her life and stay out. But he was caught up in this drama the same as the rest of them.

"He was already gone, to me, in a way. After Brad, he just disengaged from my life completely."

Adam hung his head. He'd done this to her.

Cobie drew in a ragged breath. Maybe Adam should go, after all. He'd made a mistake in coming here. He'd only opened the hurt back up.

"I need some air." She bounded up the stairs.

Adam grabbed his jacket and followed. Her friends couldn't stop him if they tried.

Cobie stood at the bow and leaned against the handrail. The wind whipped her hair around, reminding him of when she'd jumped from the bluff. A fist clenched around his heart at the reminder. He could only thank God they'd been there to pull her from the cold water.

Clouds hung heavy in the sky and turned everything gray and dark. This morning, the forecast had said it would be a beautiful day. But beautiful was in the eye of the beholder. Maybe the meteorologist liked gray and rainy.

Standing next to Cobie, Adam half expected her to lash out at him.

"I wanted to close this awful chapter of my life," she said. "That was my whole purpose in coming to the cave. And then after this, I'd planned to build something new and fresh for myself."

Adam understood that sentiment. He was shooting for the same thing. Rain started up again, sprinkling her exposed skin, clinging to her long lashes. He took off his jacket and gently hung it across her shoulders. That she didn't object surprised him.

"What do you think happened to your father?" he finally came to his reason for being here.

"I don't know. The police opened an investigation into his whereabouts. His work travel could have taken him anywhere. Sometimes I would believe he was one place only to find out he'd been a thousand miles away. I wasn't the one to call the police, of course. How could I know he was missing? I only talked to him on birthdays and Christmas."

Emotion grew thick in his throat, and he cleared it. "Who called the police then?"

"Barbara Stemmons. A woman he stayed with in Seattle. An address he called home. I've never met her. She said he hadn't come home in weeks, and she hadn't been able to contact him." Her voice sounded teary, but she stared ahead, her features hard. "The police said given his pattern, he didn't want to be found, and that was that. They're overworked and had nothing else to go on, but they would keep him listed as missing on their website, if anyone else had a lead. I can't blame them for not doing more. And I can't help but believe that I contributed to their attitude. Maybe I shouldn't have said anything. Maybe they would still be searching for him if I hadn't been so negative about the way he traveled and lived."

Adam was taken aback at her words. Clearly she was being too hard on herself. Blaming herself when she shouldn't. And her desperate need for her father's love and approval—something she might never get—rang through her words, loud and clear.

Adam said the only thing he could say. "He loved you, Cobie. You have to believe that. He just couldn't handle—"

"I know he loved me, okay? Or loves me. I can't stand to think he's gone, really gone." She swiped at another tear. "At Christmas, he told me that he wanted to make up for lost time. That he was coming back to Mountain Cove to see me, but that he had something to take care of first. I resented him for that—it was the same mantra I had heard all my life. There was always one more thing he had to do before he could make time for me. But then Barbara sent his journal to me. Said she'd found it in his things with a note from him asking her to send it to me.

"I could hear that he loved me in the words in his journal, even though he had a terrible way of showing it. He wrote that he couldn't take the pain of losing my mother when I was born, so he threw himself into his work. After Brad died, well, that was one more reason to stay away. Seeing me only reminded him of all he'd lost. I came to see the cave because he wrote about it. It was my way of being somewhere he'd been. My only way to get close to him and say goodbye. If he's dead. And maybe even if he isn't. And somehow I hope to find answers in the cave. He wrote about it as though it held some secret he wanted me to find."

For Cobie's sake, Adam hoped her father was still alive, but a sick feeling swirled inside that made him think otherwise. "Cobie, your father is missing. Maybe he wanted you to have the journal because he believed he was in danger and that he wouldn't have a chance to tell you in person how much he loved you in case something happened to him. Maybe he never meant for you to actually come to the cave, to find it. Or he could have been warning you away."

She turned to face him. The cold in her blue eyes stabbed him. "Are you suggesting that my attack today had something to do with my father, a man I haven't seen in years?"

"Maybe there's something hidden in the cave, and that's why you were attacked."

FIVE

Cobie wore some old running shoes and layered her clothes under fleece and her rain gear. She put on gloves to protect not only her hands but the cave formations from the oils in her skin that could stop stalagmite growth. She wore a headlamp attached to a helmet and carried an extra flashlight.

They waited at the slim entrance to the cave while Ray and Mel took the lead as a safety measure. After searching the island, they had concluded that her assailant had fled. Ray had taken as evidence the rock she'd used to hit the man. Thankfully, it had fallen in a sheltered spot and the rain hadn't washed it free of the blood. The slightest chance that the man had hidden in the cave remained, so Ray's reasons for going along served more than one purpose—keeping him on the job as part of his investigation, protecting them and exploring the cave with his friends the way he'd already wanted to. He hadn't asked more questions, only assured Cobie they would find her attacker.

Right. The man could have been anyone at all, out for a joy kill instead of a joyride. He could be *anywhere* by now.

Including right behind her again.

After Ray and Mel, Adam's friends, Nate, Jared and Gary, went next, readying their tape, ropes, compass, a clinometer to map the cave and a first aid kit, just in case. They seemed genuinely excited to be part of mapping the cave for the Forest Service.

But Adam hung back, studying the place where she'd run from her attacker. Since Ray and Mel had already searched that area, she wasn't sure what Adam thought he would find there. Still, it warmed her heart that he was searching. He seemed determined to keep her safe and to figure this out.

She leaned against the mossy limestone and thought back to when he and Brad had gone along with a more experienced team as novice surveyors. She hadn't realized how much donning the gear would affect her. How the memories would rush back just by seeing Adam wearing the headlamp and helmet. Only this time, Brad wasn't at his side.

The memories hurt and reminded her of the pain and anger she'd felt toward Adam all these years. But Adam—his heroic effort to save her today, his protectiveness afterward, and, yes, maybe even his sturdy form and thick hair framing his rugged, handsome face, made it hard to hold on to her re-sentiment. Being with him seemed to soften all the hardness around her heart, and her grip on her negative attitude was slowly slipping. And with that, part of her wished her friends wouldn't give him such a hard time.

Just then—as if Adam had heard her thoughts—he turned and glanced at her, then started back to them.

"Back off of Adam, okay?" she whispered to Laura.

Jared called from the cave. "Come on in, guys. Get out of the rain."

"Go ahead, Cobie," Laura said. "Jen and I will go next—then Adam can be last."

Cobie feared what her friends might say to Adam if she left them alone. Maybe she should let them have their say, but Adam had saved her life. That couldn't make up for the past—no way—but the least she could do in return was save him from her friends.

"No, you go ahead," she said. "Then Jen."

"What are you doing?" Laura angled her head, her silent question ringing loudly in Cobie's ears. *Why are you staying behind with Adam?*

"I need to talk to him alone, okay?" It was the only answer Laura would accept.

Her friend frowned. Shrugging, she slipped into the cave. Jen followed. Cobie had forgotten how overbearing Laura could be.

When Laura and Jen had disappeared inside, Adam approached. He studied her. What was he thinking? Okay, maybe she made a mistake. Maybe she didn't exactly want to be left alone with him.

"Is that true?" Adam lifted his hand as though he would reach out to her but then dropped it.

"Is what true?"

"You told Laura you needed to talk to me alone."

How did she answer that? "Um…honestly, I was protecting you."

His questioning frown shifted into that knee-weakening grin that had won her heart years ago. A mistake, she'd definitely made a mistake.

"I'm not sure what I need protection from, but I won't reject your offer."

"It's not *what*—it's *who*. I didn't want my friends to say anything to you."

His grin dropped. He scraped a hand over his face. "Yeah, they're pretty brutal. I appreciate your effort, but I can't blame your friends for their low opinion of me. They're trying to help you."

Cobie saw the question in Adam's shimmering blue eyes. All the lush greenery had turned his eyes more blue today, and they asked Cobie if *she* had a low opinion of him. She hadn't yet decided. Regardless, there could be no future for them. That much she knew. Funny how nothing much had changed there. When she was younger and Brad was still alive, she had had such a huge crush on Adam and he never once looked at her. She hadn't thought there could be a future then, either.

An odd feeling swirled up inside and rolled over the dingy walls of her heart. The way Adam looked at her now, she almost got the sense that he looked at her as more than his best friend's sister. He looked at her like a woman—a desirable woman. In all her years of dreaming about him, she'd never seen that in his eyes.

She gasped for air. "I'd better go." She made for the cave.

"Hold on, Cobie." Adam adjusted her helmet. Squatted enough to be at eye level while he did it. Why did his nearness make her insides shaky like this? She was a traitor to let the man she blamed for her brother's death affect her this way.

"What are you doing?" She moved to step away.

"Wait." He messed with the headlamp. Then he flashed her his triple-threat grin. *Oh, God, help me. I don't know if I can do this.*

Cobie swallowed. "I can take care of myself." She stepped back from him, but not nearly far enough.

"Of course you can." Adam crossed his arms. "Just like I can protect myself from your friends, but I'm not opposed to letting you fight for me."

Cobie crushed down the fierce need to express her frustration. He turned everything into playful banter, and she didn't want to play games with him.

The events of today were certainly not unfolding the way she'd expected.

Waves crashed against the rocky edges of the island, reminding her that somewhere near was the bluff she'd jumped from. Part of her wanted to back out of exploring the cave.

"Cobie, neither of us planned this today. I know being here with me, going into this cave, brings back a lot of unwanted memories. But maybe there are some good ones, too." Adam closed the distance she'd just created. "I—"

Laura slid out of the small crack in the limestone.

"You guys coming or what?" Though half her face was covered in mud, Cobie could see that Laura's eyes held concern. "Cobie? Are you sure you want to do this?"

Laura and Jen had both taken time off from their jobs and families and traveled to meet her. She'd asked a lot of them, especially since she hadn't had much contact with them since Brad's death.

"Yes. I'm sure." Cobie glanced at Adam. "I need to finish this while I'm here. And after it's over, I need to move on with my life."

Something flashed in Adam's eyes. *Regret? Hurt?* Cobie wasn't sure. When he didn't say anything, Cobie followed Laura into the cave—a dark and muddy chute that she slid down until it delivered her into a cavern. When she arrived, she was grateful for the multiple headlamps spread out like streetlights.

Cobie climbed to her feet and carefully stepped out of the slippery stream that continued twisting through the cave. Her headlamp lit up the limestone walls marbled with white and black and gray. She wanted to lay her hand over them but didn't want to cause any damage. The limestone was fragile enough she could easily chip a small piece off with one touch. Everywhere she looked, beauty and wonder met her gaze. Adam wasn't kidding about the mixed memories connected to caving, but for this moment, she tried to focus on the good ones. And make new ones.

Adam came down the chute after her and joined his friends in exploring and surveying the cave. They had work to do, after all, and Cobie would leave them to it. Jen and Laura explored the far wall of the ten-foot-tall room, and Cobie hadn't caught up to them yet.

She tried to picture her father standing here, at this very spot. Had he come to the cave in search of something for his job as a scientist, or for the sheer love of caving? If so, he hadn't mentioned either reason in his journal. He hadn't written in the journal religiously, and most of his notes were vague ramblings regarding people he met or a day on his job as an archaeologist. But most of the writing were old, except for a few notes about this cave.

Nothing that held her attention or stood out. That's why Cobie hadn't paid much attention to the fact that pages had been torn from his journal after the mention of the cave.

Maybe Adam was right to think that her father's disappearance had something to do with the man who had tried to kill her. The big question was what did this cave have to do with any of it? How long would it take them to map a caving system like this, which could have innumerable passages, loops, crawlways and rooms?

"Hey, guys," she called to Laura and Jen. "I see a room through this tight spot. Just going to explore. I'll be back up in a few." They nodded their acknowledgment.

Cobie squeezed through, her headlamp easily illuminating the next passage. She noticed a small spring emerging and water streaming away beneath the wall where she couldn't follow. And in the shadows, she saw something else.

Had someone left a pack? Was it her father's pack? Her heart skipped, and she held her breath. It couldn't be that easy. This couldn't belong to her father. She crept closer to what she thought was a pack.

Instead she found a bundle of rags. She shone her flashlight to get a better look and screamed.

The rags were clothes covering human remains.

* * *

The scream echoing through the cave walls pierced Adam's ears and sent his heart into his throat. "Cobie!"

Where had she gone? They were supposed to stick together. He ran back through the tunnels and rooms of the cave, keeping track of where he'd been, while stuffing the sketch pad into his pack. Then he slid through a tight space. Ray and Mel were close behind. They'd all gotten caught up in exploring the beauty of the unmapped cave.

Had her attacker come back?

"Someone help!" Cobie's call echoed through the tunnels. Had something happened to one of the others?

"Where are you?" he yelled.

He made the first room near the entrance, the others on his heels. Laura and Jen climbed from a crawlway.

"Here. I'm in here." Cobie's voice came from the opposite direction.

Adam followed her voice, barely managing to squeeze through the tight passage and into the room. He found her hunched over a mound, sobbing. Without thinking about his actions, he grabbed her shoulders and gently pulled her to her feet, turned her to him and into his arms.

Then he looked down at the body.

Ray and Mel had followed him in, and they

tucked away their weapons as they stood over the remains of a person long dead. Adam barely registered their words. Cobie was in his arms, after all. He needed her there, again, and this time he wanted to protect her from the world. As if Adam could actually do that. She shuddered, and he ran his hand down her back, through her hair, comforting her.

"It's hard to say how long the body's been here," Mel said. "Could have been months."

Cobie gasped against his shoulder; he thought he could feel her warm breath seeping through his rain jacket and the layers beneath meant to keep him dry.

She swiped at her eyes, shook her head and pressed her hand on his shoulder. "Sorry about that. It's just… It's just…" Cobie covered her face.

He suspected she remembered the last time she'd sobbed into his shoulder—when she'd learned that Brad had died. At the time, she hadn't known Adam's part in his death. He wanted to say more to her, but they weren't alone. Now wasn't the time. Besides, he shouldn't let his past feeling for her rise up like this. He shoved them down.

"Well, people," Mel said. "Whoever this was could have drowned. The debris along the wall near the ceiling shows the previous flood line. Or this cave could be a crime scene now."

"And we'll treat it as such until we know different," Ray said.

A thick knot, gnarled with pain and guilt, lodged

in Adam's throat. Adam and Brad had been in a cave when Brad drowned. That had been an accident. A foolish mistake, but an accident. He let his arms drop when Cobie moved away. He glanced up to the gunk left near the ceiling—the signature of a recent waterline—that Mel had pointed out. This cave had flooded at some point. Had the water washed the body here? Nausea roiled at the thought, at the sight of the body.

"Why do you say that?" Adam asked. "Couldn't it have been an accident?"

"Do you think the same man who attacked Cobie killed this man?" Jen asked.

Ray shook his head, the light from his helmet swathing across the cave with his action. This stunning underground world was destroyed by the sight of death. "No way to know if this is related. But we can be sure this didn't happen anytime recently."

"You said this could be a crime scene." Jared crossed his arms. "What makes you think this man was murdered? Like Adam said, couldn't it have been an accident?"

"I can't know for sure how he died. But he's not wearing the equipment he would need to traverse this cave alone. There's no flashlight or headlamp. I don't think he came here alone. Someone came with him or forced him inside. Either way they left him here. Or he was washed up from another room." Ray scraped a hand over his face. "Investigating this is going to be a mess. From this point on, touch nothing else."

"Wait, are you saying we can't map the cave?" Nate had garnered this opportunity from the Forest Service to begin with; he would feel this loss the most.

"That's what I'm saying. Until we know more."

To everyone's surprise, Cobie bent down and lifted something from the body.

"Cobie, what are you doing?" Ray demanded. "Don't touch anything."

She held up a ring dangling from a chain, grief evident in her features. Instead of answering Ray, she looked at Adam and held his gaze as though the two of them were the only ones in the cave, in the world.

"These clothes, they're what my father always wore. And he always wore this ring on a chain around his neck. It was my mother's."

SIX

Cobie's words echoed against the cave walls as shock ricocheted through Adam's core.

No one moved or spoke. Everyone stared at her. At the ring dangling from a chain, dancing in the light of multiple headlamps.

"You sure?" Ray took a step closer.

She closed her fingers around the ring, nodding in response. She hung her head, her quiet weeping now the only sound.

Adam wanted to go to her, but waited for Ray's response.

"We're going to need that for the investigation." Ray gestured for Adam to comfort her.

Adam closed the short distance and put his arm around Cobie, drawing her near again, though he felt helpless to reassure her. Neither of them could have imagined this, the worst possible outcome. At the very least, it should have been Adam who found the remains so he could protect her from that image. Bad enough to learn her father was actually dead.

"Cobie." Ray stood next to them, his voice gentle as he repeated his earlier words. "We're going to need the ring and the chain for our investigation."

Adam shared a look with Ray. They both knew she wouldn't willingly release it. And sure enough, she held on all the tighter. Adam held her tighter, too, and eyed Ray. His friend backed off. He could get the ring later.

In the meantime, Adam would hold Cobie in his arms as long as she needed. For eternity, if necessary. Pressing her forehead against his chest, she clenched his jacket in her fists, along with the ring, and cried, angry sobs mixed with the deepest, soul-piercing sorrow and regret. Reminding Adam all over again of the day Brad had died.

He squeezed his eyes shut, held Cobie to him, afraid to let her go. *Why, God? Why is this happening again?*

Cobie had come for answers, and she'd gotten at least one. But finding her father like this created even more questions.

Before Adam realized what was happening, Laura and Jen pulled Cobie from his arms and into theirs, ushering her out of the small room where her father's body had been found, and putting Adam in his place.

Just as well. He had no business attempting to comfort her. Her friends were more suitable for the task, so Adam buried his anguish and went to see how he could assist Ray and busy himself until this experience was behind him.

On the beach, Adam tossed his bag into Billy's seaplane, which he'd maneuvered right up to the sand. After Adam placed Cobie's bags inside, he turned and shook Billy's hand.

"Thanks for coming on such short notice, man."

"Not a problem." Billy tugged on his Mountain Cove Air ball cap, his expression somber. "This isn't out of my way, and even if it was, you know I'd come for you. I came back earlier to check on Cobie and saw she wasn't alone, so left it at that."

"I appreciate it. It's not that I couldn't leave with Gary, but—"

"You don't have to explain." Billy continued readying his plane to take Cobie and Adam back home.

Mountain Cove.

He hadn't planned on going back until, well, Christmas. It had been hard enough to leave as it was. He'd finally worked up his nerve to explore the world outside Alaska, and losing his business to the fire had given him the perfect opportunity— freedom. He didn't have a business to tie him down anymore.

And then today had happened.

His friends stood on the beach, talking to Ray and Mel. Cobie still huddled with Laura and Jen a few yards away, saying goodbye to her friends. She looked better. The color was back in her cheeks. Her friends had bolstered her, probably in a way Adam never could, so for that, he was thankful they'd come. Grateful they'd interfered with his attempts to comfort her upon discovering her father's body. But they would leave her behind today when they headed back to their homes and lives in Laura's boat, and Cobie would fly back to Mountain Cove with Billy.

And Adam, though she didn't know that yet.

Nate, Jared and Gary wanted to stop on another island and explore another cave, maybe survey it, too. Regret hung around Adam's neck for the horrible way this planned trip had turned out, pulling him down until he thought he would simply fall flat on his face and quit trying to move forward and on with his life.

If this were about any other woman except Cobie, Adam would go with his friends and try to forget the past. Then he'd follow through on the plans that would take him away from life in Alaska. That's what he wanted. Or thought he had wanted until Cobie stepped back into his life.

I don't know what you're doing here, God, if anything. Adam didn't know what *he* was doing, either. *But I could use some direction, some guidance in all of this.*

Regardless of how they each felt about their past,

Cobie took priority over his plans. For her brother's sake. Brad would have wanted Adam to watch out for her. Knowing that, he felt a little bad that he'd kept his distance all these years—except that was the way Cobie had wanted it. Kind of hard to do in a small town, but they had somehow managed.

Today had changed everything for them both.

Someone had tried to kill her. And if that wasn't enough, she had found what she believed was her father's body.

From Adam's perspective, it was all part of the same big nightmare.

He hiked over to his friends and said his good-byes. They lived in Mountain Cove, and he'd see them on the other end of their caving. They headed back to the trawler in the skiff.

Ray nodded a farewell, his expression serious. "We'll be in touch, Adam. This isn't over yet. I'll be in touch with the state police, too."

"What about Cobie?"

Ray's gaze swung over to her. "Any way you can stay close? Watch out for her? I'll give Chief Winters a call and fill him in so nothing will blindside him. It's all I can do at this juncture."

Adam pursed his lips, nodded his understanding. "Keep me updated?"

"Will do."

Ray and Mel headed to their own boat. Adam didn't know how they would handle the body, but he needed to push that image out of his mind. He was grateful Ray had been there and would take things from here. Adam stood on the beach and studied the island and the marine fog moving in and growing thick. Billy was probably eager to leave.

Finally, Laura and Jen waved goodbye to Cobie. She hung her head, and Laura ran back to her and hugged her again. *Come on, people. Skype or something.* Adam wanted to get out of there. Get Cobie out of there.

When she whirled to face the plane, he could see her eyes remained red and puffy. But what had he expected? It would take time to get over the trauma of the last few hours. He stiffened when he saw her study the beach, the slow realization crossing her face that Billy had two passengers to fly back to Mountain Cove.

He half expected her to come over and yell at him to go away, leave her alone, but instead Cobie marched over to the plane where Billy waited and climbed into the seat next to the pilot. Billy gave Adam a look through the window. *What are you waiting for, dummy?*

Nerves. That's all it was. He didn't know what Cobie would think about him riding back with her, but surely she saw that logically it made the most sense. But after the emotional roller coaster they'd been through, he doubted logic was holding much sway with either of them just now.

How could everything have gotten so completely messed up? How had things gone so wrong between him and the woman he'd dreamed about for so long? And see? That he was thinking about *that* said what a self-centered jerk he was. His only concern should be her well-being. Maybe that was the problem—he could hardly stand to think how she'd been hurt today. It squashed him. And if it squashed *him*, what was it doing to her?

Adam climbed into the seat behind Cobie and strapped in. Billy started up the seaplane, steered it out of the cove and took off. The whir of the props made conversation difficult, but the man usually talked over the noise anyway. Admittedly, it drained Adam, who'd much rather look out the windows and silently enjoy the view. But this time he would have welcomed the idle chitchat. The silence—except for the buzzing vibration of the prop—was deafening.

Billy steered the plane around the misty island, flying close. Adam absently studied what had held such beauty for him until today.

Through a break in the mist, Adam spotted a man staring up from the island, watching the plane.

The plane bucked against the turbulence, banking left, then right, dropping abruptly. Cobie's stomach rolled with the fuselage. Focused, Billy stared ahead. Behind her, she knew that, like her, Adam stayed lost in his own thoughts.

Rain pelted the plane, and she watched rivulets forming on the window next to her. Squeezing her eyes shut, Cobie tried to shove away the images, the nightmare of the day. A futile effort.

She hadn't seen the man Adam claimed to have seen on the island. By the time she'd glanced out her window, the mist had shifted, the plane had moved and he'd disappeared. Was it the same man who'd tried to kill her today?

And what of her father?

Hold it together—just hold it together. She didn't want to lose it front of Billy and Adam.

Adam hadn't been able to reach Ray to let him know about spotting someone on the island when they had thought it was deserted. Of course, whoever was there might not have a thing to do with her attacker, but they'd been the only ones on the island that afternoon. Or so they'd believed.

Finally, the Mountain Cove seaplane dock came into view. Cobie almost felt as if she'd been holding her breath, waiting to see it. Once the plane was secured at the dock, she helped Billy and Adam remove the bags. All she wanted was to get into her Explorer and go home.

Billy helped stash her things in the back. "Hey, you don't need to do this. I got it," she said.

He gave her a somber look. "You're welcome."

Ah. Nailed. "Thank you." She should have been

grateful instead of trying to be so self-sufficient. But she'd had years of practice.

Billy stepped aside, and Adam tossed yet another bag into the backseat. They probably wondered why she'd packed so much. She'd just wanted to be prepared. But nothing could have prepared her for today.

"If you guys don't think you need me anymore, I have another errand to run." Billy quirked a grin.

"We're good, Billy, thanks," Adam said.

Billy nodded, tipped his cap and strolled back to his seaplane.

"*We're* good?" she asked.

"Didn't mean anything by it. Just letting Billy know I'm here to help you so he can go."

"I don't want or need your help." What did he think he was doing?

She didn't want him stepping back into her life just because they'd been thrown into another nightmare together. Cobie left Adam standing there, marched around the other side of her vehicle and got in. She started the ignition. Hung her head. She shouldn't have been so rude. But today had been difficult enough. And yet, wouldn't she be disappointed if he hadn't at least tried to help? To check on her? Make sure she was okay?

When she dared to look up, he was gone. He hadn't tried very hard. Cobie steered out of the parking lot and headed back to her house tucked in a nice neighborhood not too far from her dentist office. Five minutes later, she parked the Explorer in the driveway. She'd become a dentist because it would give her stability, and she could buy her own home and stay in Mountain Cove. Her father's career had sent him traveling, working for weeks at a time miles away from home, leaving his two children behind with a nanny. She didn't want that. She wouldn't follow in his footsteps, just as she'd always told him. The next time they spoke, she'd— And, oh…wow… He was dead. Really dead.

Even though he hadn't been a part of her life in so long, his death was hard to comprehend, especially when it seemed as though he'd wanted to take steps to reconnect. She hadn't trusted his words, but they had made her want to believe. Oh, how she'd wanted to believe she would have the chance to get to know him again, to spend time with him. She could never get back those lost years, and that's what she'd come to think of them as—lost years— but they could have made some new memories. That had all ended when he went missing. Today, any hope of a future that included her father had died with the sight of his body.

He'd written about exploring the cave in his journal, though he hadn't said why—was it work related? Was he looking for something archaeological?

Had he found something inside that had cost him

his life? But Cobie wouldn't figure that out today. She realized she'd been sitting in her driveway, the engine running. The house was dark, and she was alone. What an idiot she'd been to run Adam off. Her short words to him came back to mock her now.

I don't want or need your help.

Whoever had tried to kill her today, surely they didn't know where she lived. How could they? No one even knew she was going to be on the island, other than Laura and Jen. How could her attack have anything to do with her father being dead inside the cave? But how could it not?

She pressed her face into her hands. There wasn't any way she could think through it all without some serious rest and food and...distance. Perspective would go a long way in helping her contextualize everything that had happened. And then she'd go see Chief Winters and tell him everything, even though none of it had happened within the Mountain Cove PD jurisdiction. Still, he needed to know. In case something did happen here.

There was nothing for it. She was being a chicken with a big *C*. She got out of her vehicle. If she could wish for anything, it would be that she'd gotten home before the sun had gone down. But she shouldn't need sunlight to feel safe in her own home. Mountain Cove had always been a relatively safe place to live. No one dared to try to hurt another because almost everyone carried a weapon. Lots of people. And that's why Cobie didn't find it necessary.

But first thing tomorrow she would at least get herself a stun gun.

Lights flashed as a vehicle headed up the street, illuminating her as she walked up the sidewalk to her front door. That was enough light to see no one waited in the shadows. She unlocked the door, flipped on the outside lights and then the inside lights and stepped inside. Her knees buckled at the sight that greeted her.

SEVEN

Adam parked, then jumped out of his truck. He jogged up the sidewalk to Cobie's house, unsure what to expect. Would she be angry that he'd followed her? Maybe. But he wouldn't let her push him away. Not now. What kind of friend would he be to let her sit home alone when someone had tried to kill her? Maybe she didn't want him as a friend anymore, but he would be there for her anyway.

"For Brad," he whispered to himself. "Cobie!" He quickened his pace.

The front door stood open, and the light from the porch chased away some of the darkness around the house. Cobie stood in the foyer, framed by the open door. Adam made it onto the porch and lingered on the other side of the threshold. Beyond Cobie, he could see what kept her frozen in place.

"I'm here." *Forgive me. I should have been here all along. That's what friends are for.*

"Oh, Adam."

He observed the damage—furniture overturned,

bookshelves toppled, papers scattered. "We should leave. We don't know—"

A noise sounded from somewhere in the house.

"You have to get out of here." Adam yanked her through the door and off the porch, then ushered her across the street toward his truck. His gaze searching the area for imminent danger, he tugged out his weapon and prepared for the worst. With Cobie in his grip, he opened the truck passenger-side door. "Get in."

Cobie didn't argue, but climbed into his truck. "What should I do?"

"Call the police. I'm going to drive up the road a little."

"What? I can't just leave someone inside my house so they can tear everything up."

"Yes, you absolutely can if there's any chance that that person might try to harm you. A man tried to kill you today. Now someone is in your house, searching for something. It's too risky to try and threaten them or scare them out of the house."

Adam didn't wait for Cobie's agreement. He started the truck and peeled from the curb while she called 9-1-1 and reported a burglar. Adam whipped the truck around and shone the lights on her home. They were at a safe distance, and this way they could watch the house. See what they would see.

He made sure the doors on the truck were locked, and he watched the mirrors so no one could sneak up on them from behind. He didn't want to think about what could have happened if he hadn't shown up. Maybe nothing, or maybe someone would have tried to kill her again. They might have succeeded this time.

"Thank you for coming here tonight," she whispered. "I know what I said back there at the seaplane dock was rude. And I'm sorry."

"No need to apologize. I understand what you meant beneath the words. You're strong and don't need me to babysit you. I shouldn't have taken offense." Had he just admitted he had? "But you should know I had every intention of seeing you home safely tonight, with or without your permission. Unfortunately, I got a little delayed, but not by much. I'm glad I was here."

She laughed softly.

He angled his head at her. *Really?* She could laugh? "What's so funny?"

"That's the most I've ever heard you say at once." She smiled. Incredibly, she smiled.

He couldn't believe she'd found a smile within her after the day she'd had. But he knew his words had been true—she was one of the strongest people he knew, and she would reach down inside and do what she needed to do to survive.

The sound of sirens ripped through the night, and lights flashed from two cruisers as one pulled up to the curb and the other into the driveway behind

Cobie's car. Adam slowly steered up to the house and lowered his window.

Officer Terry Stratford jogged up to the truck. He peered inside. "You reported someone was inside your house?"

"Yes." Cobie leaned closer to Adam to speak to Terry. "And they could still be there."

"She had an attempt made on her life already today, Terry," Adam added. "We're not going inside until you check it out. They were still there when we arrived."

Terry nodded and issued instructions to the other officers, which included drawing their weapons. Adam reached over and grabbed Cobie's hand, held it and squeezed. She didn't pull away. He thought he'd hold her hand to comfort her, bolster her, but as it turned out, he drew strength from her. That was a problem. He hadn't known he needed reassurance. Worse, he had a feeling the kind of assurance he needed could only come from Cobie.

At the end of this week he was supposed to board a plane in Juneau and head to Texas. He still wanted to get on that plane. He *needed* that time away for a hundred reasons. He'd dreamed of this chance, this one chance, to escape his guilt and his memories. But how could he leave Cobie in the middle of this ordeal?

He didn't have the answers. He hoped to have them by the end of the week.

Together, he and Cobie waited silently for something to happen: The police to return with someone in custody. Or someone to flee the house. Adam held his breath and figured Cobie probably did, too. If they caught whoever had been in the house, could be they'd have her attacker from earlier today and it would all be over. Adam would have his answer—he could board that plane and leave his brief encounter with her behind him.

Two of the policemen, including Terry, exited the house. Terry marched over to the pickup. "The house is empty."

He peered over Adam at Cobie. "Whoever was inside was looking for something. That much is obvious. But you scared them off before they finished. Instead of searching your bedroom, looks like they climbed out the window. You're not going to want to stay here tonight. But come inside and see if you can identify anything missing."

Cobie nodded and tried to pull her hand away, but Adam held on. With all that had happened today she had to be in shock. He'd give her whatever support she'd accept.

"You don't have to, if you don't want to," Adam said.

Terry didn't say otherwise.

"I want to see, Adam. I'm okay."

He released her hand and watched her climb out of the truck. He did the same. As Terry walked with her, Adam glanced at the surrounding homes and woods across the way. Was the burglar still out there watching? Was it the same man who'd tried to kill her? Or was it an accomplice?

I'm still in the same nightmare. When will I ever wake up?

Cobie stumbled through her living room, two police officers flanking her. Her antique accent chest was filleted, the drawers emptied, sofa and chairs ripped. Someone hadn't cared if she knew they'd been in her house. But then maybe they'd been in a hurry.

She glanced at Adam; his expression looked as stricken as hers must. "I don't understand. What were they looking for?"

"Are, Cobie," he said. "What *are* they looking for. Someone searched your bags at the cabin, too, remember?"

She had kind of hoped the two incidents weren't related, but at this point she would be lying to herself if she believed otherwise. That meant someone knew she'd be at the cave and knew that she wasn't home. Her pulse skipped. What was going on?

"See anything missing?" Terry asked.

"I don't know. It's hard to say without taking time to look through every detail."

"Take your time then."

Cobie's home was small and cozy, and she'd

stuffed it with furnishings, tapestries and beautiful collectibles and antiques, all in an attempt to fill the empty places. Having someone break in and destroy those things in a place she'd believed was a safe haven from the world outside shook her to the core. The mess prevented her from seeing anything obviously missing.

The extra bedroom appeared moderately searched, as if the thief had known he was running out of time. In her bedroom nothing was askew except the open window with the dislodged screen. That must have been the noise she and Adam had heard—the burglar making his escape.

"Is it okay if I close this?" She looked at Terry.

"Leave it for now. Got someone coming to dust for prints."

Cobie frowned. *What is he after?* "How long will it take before I can stay here again?"

"Ask me again tomorrow. Since Adam mentioned you've been through something similar today already, it's possible that the two incidents could be related. Please come by the police station in the morning and we'll take your statement. In the meantime, do you have someplace safe to stay tonight?"

Heaviness weighed on her shoulders. Cobie dropped to the edge of her bed. She'd grown up in this town. She should have more friends, but she'd thrown herself into her work. The two close friendships she'd had ran deep, but both of those people had moved away. The only family she'd had left—her brother and her father—was now deceased. Could she really be this alone? Caught up in her work, in a business she'd built to keep her roots deep in one place, she hadn't put the time and effort into relationships. In the end, she was more like her father had been than she was ready to admit.

"Yes," Adam said.

Cobie jerked her gaze to him. He wasn't suggesting—

"My grandmother." Adam's blue-green eyes shimmered with compassion and a slice of humor, too.

"Oh no, that would be too much trouble. I can't impose on her. I can stay at a hotel, or maybe the Jewel of the Mountain bed-and-breakfast has an extra room." But she didn't want to drive that far out.

"Grandma Katy has plenty of extra rooms since everyone moved out. You know she would enjoy the company. She loves to take care of people."

"I don't need taking care of."

He drew closer, took her hand and pulled her to her feet, as if police officers weren't waiting. Watching. "Humor me. I don't want you to stay alone tonight. Grandma… She bakes cookies and makes you feel all warm and cozy. Come on, after the day you've had, you could go for some of that tender loving care about now, couldn't you?"

Terry cleared his throat. "You might bring some of those cookies with you to the station tomorrow. Just saying…"

Was everyone ganging up on her? Cobie wasn't sure how she felt about that. How she felt about any of it. She couldn't think clearly enough. If she checked into a hotel, she'd just lie awake all night. She had too much to process. And she wouldn't be able to sleep because she would also be afraid.

"What if someone tries to come after me again? I don't want to put your grandmother in danger."

"No one is going to get within a hundred yards of my grandmother's house." Adam dropped her hand and moved to the window. He frowned as he peered out into the night.

It was obvious her words had gotten to him.

"Between me and Adam," Terry said, "we can watch over the house. That is, unless Chief Winters decides the police needs an official presence. Then we can still stand guard tonight. You want my unofficial opinion, you should take Adam up on his suggestion and stay with his grandmother instead of checking into a hotel. But it's up to you, of course." Terry exited the room, leaving her to make the decision. His partner followed.

Cobie stood alone with Adam. She could never have imagined that she would be in a situation like this, and with Adam no less.

"What are you doing here, Adam? You're not ob-

ligated to be here with me or to watch over me tonight like Terry suggested. I didn't mean to involve
you in any of this."

He jammed his hands into his jeans. "I'm involved. Neither of us has to like it."

EIGHT

While Cobie was upstairs unpacking, Adam filled his grandmother in. Her features appeared bright and lively as she pulled together leftovers to create an aromatic soup. He regretted they'd all moved out, leaving her alone. His personal guilt was especially strong. At least his siblings had left to get married and start families. Adam had moved out just to be on his own. Maybe it was that same restlessness that was driving him to leave Alaska and travel to parts unseen.

He focused his thoughts on his grandmother.

She thrived on serving people. At least she had plenty of friends and ministry outreach opportunities through Mountain Cove Community Church, but Adam was certain that wasn't enough to keep her from getting lonely. That was part of the reason he'd suggested Cobie stay here. He was certain that if she'd had any other choice besides a hotel or the local B and B, she would have taken it.

It was a tough balancing act. Keeping his attitude

warm and friendly while protecting his heart. He also had to maintain enough distance that he didn't chase her away and yet keep her close. Cobie needed friends right now, and protection, and it was an odd set of events that had given him the job.

Grandma Katy stirred the contents of her large stockpot and shook her head. "I'm glad you brought her here, Adam. I'll take care of her."

Adam leaned against the counter, expecting Cobie to come down the stairs any minute. "Don't count on her to stay long. She's pretty independent and will want to get back into her house as soon as possible."

Grandma stopped stirring and cocked a brow at Adam. "And how safe would that be, staying there alone with a madman out there?"

Try at least two madmen. No way could the same guy have been in both places. "I don't know. I just don't know."

Adam brushed his hand over his whiskers. He needed a shower and shave, but he wasn't ready to leave.

"I think it would be obvious what this man is after. Maybe not to you, but you're a character in the story. Let's say I'm reading this story."

Cobie appeared then at the bottom of the steps, looking tired but a little fresher. "What's obvious?"

"The journal, dear. He or she is after your father's journal."

"Makes sense." Adam crossed his arms, studying Cobie. He wasn't just humoring his grandmother—it really was something to think about. He'd already mentioned to Cobie that her father might have been trying to communicate something about the cave. That maybe something was hidden inside. Or perhaps he wanted to warn her away. But then why bring it up? Unless he'd planned to write more and never had the chance? Too much had happened in the span of a short time and neither of them were thinking clearly. His grandmother, on the other hand, was looking at things with a set of fresh eyes.

Cobie's blue eyes shot to him. Those eyes had been his weakness from the beginning. He thought about them often.

Chewing on her lip, Cobie slid onto a stool at the counter. "I don't agree."

Satisfied her concoction had cooked long enough, Grandma Katy ladled out servings of soup and handed a bowl each to Adam and Cobie. "I spend most of my evenings reading mysteries this last couple of years since the kids have moved out." She glanced up, a small smile gracing her lips. "I say kids, but Heidi and Cade have been adults for more than a decade now. Just because they got married didn't mean they needed to move out. Adam and David moved out before those two."

She tossed him an admonishing look.

Adam wrapped his hands round the steaming

soup bowl, breathed in the aroma. His stomach rumbled. Grandma had taken the conversation elsewhere, but if he gave her enough time, she'd bring it back. He wrapped his mouth around a big heaping spoon of hot soup created from something meaty and lots of veggies, beans and pasta, and listened.

"Of course, I don't understand why Adam is still single. That's the only reason he'd ever leave Mountain Cove—because he doesn't have a reason to stay. Instead, he'll go on this cockamamy world-traveling tour all by himself."

Uh-oh. He set his bowl down. She was taking the conversation places he didn't want to go.

Grandma patted Cobie's hand. "But look at you, you've given him a reason to stay."

She locked her gaze with Adam's. He didn't know how to rescue either of them. "You were leaving Mountain Cove? Going on a world tour? And you're not going to do that now because of *me*?"

"Oh, what have I done? We can't eat soup without crackers." Grandma set out the crackers. "There, that's better. Now, tell me why you don't think it's the journal they're after."

Adam had no idea if his grandmother recognized her faux pas and intentionally pulled the conversation back or what, but he breathed a sigh of relief. He could see in Cobie's eyes that he wasn't off the hook and would have to explain things to her, but he was grateful for the temporary reprieve. The truth was he hadn't decided if he would leave or stay. He hoped they would find her attacker and put him away, but if that didn't happen by the end of the week, there was no way he would keep his travel plans. In that case, he would have a lot of cancellation phone calls to make, and he would probably lose some significant money, too.

So be it. Cobie's safety was more important.

"I've read it," Cobie insisted. "There's nothing in the journal that's a secret. Nothing of importance. There are pages missing, torn out at the end, sure, but given the kind of thing he wrote in the journal, I imagine it was just more of the same. In fact, I'm not sure why he even kept a journal. I don't see why he wanted me to have it."

That seemed to slow Grandma Katy up. "I...see."

After tasting the soup again, her face twisted up. She moved back to the stockpot and seasoned the soup with additional salt, pepper and other herbs, then gave it another taste. She smiled again. "Your next bowl should be better."

"I'm sorry. I didn't mean to throw a rotten carrot into your mystery solving, but that can't be it," Cobie added.

"Where *is* the journal, Cobie?" Adam asked. "Is it in the bags you brought with you?"

She pulled in a long breath. "No, it's at the house."

Adam couldn't stand to see his grandmother's

disappointment. "Are you sure about that? Did you see it there after the burglar left?"

Cobie stared into her soup. "No. I wasn't looking for it. There was too much of a mess, and I didn't think of it."

Anger twisted in Adam's gut to think that her father might have put her in danger by leaving her the journal. It didn't make sense that he would put her at risk intentionally. But what had the man been thinking? He should have known better than to have the journal sent to her. If that was the connection at all. Had her father's friend who sent her the journal experienced any break-ins?

"There must be a clue inside the journal, and that's why he left it with you." Grandma Katy began cleaning up the dishes. Storing away the soup. "You and Adam should see if you can find it tomorrow."

Except Adam was more than positive they would not find the journal inside Cobie's house. And if it was gone, then good riddance and maybe this would all be over for Cobie.

Two days later, Cobie headed into her office for her first day back at work. Yesterday she'd told her story to a mildly interested detective. The night of the break-in, Officer Stratford had made it sound as if the police would be interested to hear about the strange events of her day. But he hadn't been there and neither had Chief Winters, and the detective who had taken her statement had been blasé about the idea that she might be in danger. Then she'd spent the rest of the day cleaning up the mess the intruder had made in her house. The fingerprint dust was almost worse than the papers strewn everywhere, worse than her ripped furniture. She also waited for the insurance adjuster to come look at the damage. There was really no reason why the thief needed to rip apart her furniture. What did he think she would have hidden there?

Not the journal. She'd placed it in the back of a drawer in the desk. Why wouldn't someone look there first? Except they hadn't been after the journal at all, clearly. It was still in the drawer.

At any rate, she hadn't slept at home last night, and was still at Katy's house. But tonight, well, she should sleep in her own home. The cleaning would go faster that way. But she wasn't nearly as put out by that as by her experience at the police department.

Frustration pooled in her veins as she drove her Explorer down Main Street and thought about the time she'd wasted with the detective. The man hadn't raised a brow or questioned her further. But her father's cause of death wasn't the Mountain Cove PD's concern because the body had not been found within their jurisdiction, nor did he live here. Cobie was a Mountain Cove resident, but she'd been attacked elsewhere. Cobie could only hope that

Adam's LEI agent friend, Ray, would stay on top of things from his end and perhaps connect with Chief Winters. The break-in at her house was the Mountain Cove PD's priority, though they still didn't know what the person was looking for.

Cobie wished she had kept their suspicions over the journal to herself, after she and Adam found it untouched. But it seemed strange that after receiving the journal, she'd ventured to the cave mentioned in the journal, was assaulted and found her father's body. This she'd shared with the detective, who'd assured her he would share it with the other law enforcement entities involved.

All she'd wanted was closure. Well, she had found a version of it when she'd found her father's body. At least now she knew why he hadn't been in touch the way he'd said he would. She wanted to know if someone had murdered him like they'd tried to murder her. She should give Ray a call and find out who to contact. When the medical examiner would know something.

After steering into the parking lot of her small dental practice, she parked in the farthest spot from the office to give her patients and employees the closer spots.

She was going crazy and wanted to scream. This was why she needed to work and focus on someone else's problems today. Her staff—receptionist and appointment scheduler, insurance and billing and one of two hygienists—had kept things running while she'd taken time off. She wouldn't lose clients if she stayed away today, but she needed to get her mind on something else. And Adam's grandmother, despite being kind and welcoming, would smother her if she stayed there. That much she knew.

She entered the office through the front door. Passing through the waiting area, she noticed two clients reading. She shoved through the door to the hallway. Dana sat at the receptionist's desk on the phone and her eyes grew wide when she noticed Cobie, but Cobie simply waved and kept going. She passed two empty dental chairs. In the last room, her hygienist Kelly had a client in a chair, cleaning his teeth. Cobie wouldn't bother her. She unlocked her office door, and relief hit her. She'd half expected to find her office ransacked, as well. But it was the same as always—professional. Neat. Clean. Diplomas and certificates of her achievements were hanging on the wall. This almost felt more like home to her than her actual home did, especially now that it was in disarray. That she'd scared off an intruder made her skin crawl.

She closed the door behind her, flipped on the lights and sat in the chair at her desk. Might as well go through the mail that Dana had stacked on her desk while she was gone. She'd need to coordinate with Barbara to make funeral arrangements for her father, too, as soon as they released his body.

A pang seized her heart. She could hardly believe that he was really gone. She hadn't realized how tightly she'd held on to a small hope that one day they could build a real relationship.

Chucking some of the junk mail in the small trash receptacle, she noticed a handwritten card addressed to her. Using her letter opener, she tore the envelope and slid out a card. A s*ympathy* card? She ignored the words meant to comfort and skipped to the signature. Dr. Yuri Burkov, one of her father's colleagues, an anthropologist and professor at the University of Alaska Southeast had sent this yesterday. How in the world had he learned about her father's death so soon? They hadn't even officially identified the body.

Cobie picked up the phone and called the university, hoping to speak with Dr. Burkov or at least leave a message. She needed to meet with him. Find out when he'd last spoken to her father. She remembered her father mentioning his friend often and Cobie had had the pleasure of meeting him when her father had taken her and Brad to Juneau with him to see Yuri. The two men had been close. As she listened to the phone ring, she realized she wanted to speak to Dr. Burkov for another reason. She wanted to hear a few stories about her father. If only she had tried harder to be part of his life, whether he wanted it or not.

They said hindsight was twenty-twenty. If she

was smart, she'd take this lesson and learn from it. Spend time with important people while she had the chance. But she'd already lost almost everyone important to her, and those who were left… Her thoughts jumped right to Adam, except that relationship wasn't meant to be. Could never happen.

NINE

Adam pulled into the parking lot in time to see the staff exiting. His grandmother had called to inform him that Cobie planned to sleep in her own home tonight. Of course, he couldn't force her to stay at his grandmother's. She had to go home at some point, and he was probably overstepping by coming here as it was. But on the other hand, he'd never forgive himself if something happened to her when she was on her own and unprotected. She shouldn't be alone until they caught the guy who'd tried to kill her. He'd already charged himself with the responsibility of keeping her safe.

He'd kept his distance today while she worked—she should be safe enough there—and spent his time bugging Chief Winters about the investigation. That, and helping his brother Cade on some reports he planned to use for a class he was teaching at the avalanche center as they geared up for the winter season.

Adam parked next to Cobie's Explorer and slid out

of his truck, figuring it would be easier to talk her into going back to Grandma Katy's house tonight than it would be to talk her into leaving her home once she got there and dug in. He'd planned to intercept her at closing time. He was being a little manipulative here, but he couldn't help feeling that he'd been put in the position to help her through this horrible time. Some cosmic plan had been orchestrated to force him back into Cobie's life. Who was he to argue with that?

Trudging forward, he watched the staff leave and eyed Cobie's empty vehicle. He didn't like that she was in the office alone and would tell her as much. When he got to the door, he tried to shove through, but it was locked. The lights in the front office had been turned off. Adam knocked, almost wishing he had a medical reason to see her—like a toothache— but that wouldn't get him in to see her tonight.

Through the glass door, Adam watched as Cobie appeared in the hallway, a frown fighting a curious smile. She headed toward the door with her key.

Instead of fully opening the door and inviting him in, she cracked it. "Adam, what are you doing here?" Her frown lingered a moment, and then her eyes softened. "What's happened?"

"Nothing. Do you mind if I come in?"

Another grimace and then she swung the door open.

Adam stepped inside. "I just came by to make sure you're okay."

At her look he held his hands up in a defensive shrug. "I know you can take care of yourself, Cobie."

She locked the door behind him and headed down the hallway. "You can come on back if you want."

In her office, she sat behind her desk. Adam took the seat across from it. Cobie stared at her computer screen, obviously caught up in her work. She made sure he knew he'd interrupted her, and that made him feel more like an idiot with each passing minute. She typed quickly on the keyboard and glanced over at him as she did, a hint of a smile finally surfacing. "Sorry, just trying to catch up on a few things."

"Can't you do that during the day while you're surrounded with people? I don't think you should be here alone after dark."

Cobie stared at the screen, then shut down the computer. She turned her full attention on him. She looked much better than she had since this ordeal had begun. Staying at his grandmother's—with the sturdy meals and the warmth and comfort—had been good for Cobie. There was more color in her cheeks, and her sweet, full lips fought to keep from spreading into a full-on smile; he could tell. Those big blues stared back at him, studied him, as she visibly considered how to reply.

He knew she didn't like him interfering, but he thought he saw something else behind her gaze.

Something he'd always wanted to see. He thought he saw that she was glad to see him.

"When we got back from the island, I told you I didn't want or need your help. I started to say that again, but, Adam…it isn't true. I don't know what I would have done without you. Without your grandmother letting me stay with her. But I don't want to take advantage of her good nature. So that's why I'm going home tonight. I'm guessing that's why you stopped by. You thought you could talk me into staying."

The woman knew him too well.

He grinned, but he wasn't ready to give in. He needed more time to convince her. "How about I take you to dinner and we can talk about it?"

She swept her long brown mane back away from her face and wrapped a band around it, then blew out a breath. "I have so much work to do. I can't tonight, I'm sorry. Rain check?"

"We'll drive through and grab fast food, and I'll help you clean up the house."

Shaking her head, she got up. "Adam, I can't do this with you."

"What? I'm offering to help. That's all. And you admitted you needed my help."

She turned her back on him and straightened a certificate that hung askew. "I need some time to think through everything alone. And you… Adam, you should go on your trip."

As she faced him, he saw that the hurt and resentment had returned to her eyes. "Don't stay on my account. Don't help me out of some strange obligation to my brother."

The pain rose up in his throat, thick and full, burning him like the tears had that day. He'd wanted a chance to tell her again that he was sorry for everything, for his part in her brother's death. And now he had that chance. Only the words wouldn't come out like he'd planned. "You still hold that against me, don't you? How many times do I have to say I'm sorry?"

Moisture pooled and shimmered in her eyes, making them look all the bigger, all the bluer. "I'm trying, okay? But I've been through a lot in the last few days, and all of it reminds me of him and of that day."

And of Adam's part in it.

Shame filled him for pushing her, and he shoved his head down, keeping his gaze on the carpeted floor. "That's understandable."

"Give me some time, okay?" Cobie croaked out the words as she gathered her coat and purse.

They would never get past this, and he wasn't sure if he wanted to try. Hadn't he told himself he wouldn't go through this again? "I told myself I was protecting you for Brad's sake, but honestly I don't think that's the truth. And I don't know if I can leave unless I know that you're going to be safe. That this is over. So there's that. Maybe you can tolerate my presence a little longer, until we end this and I know you're out of danger."

Adam lifted his gaze and captured hers, held it long and hard, delivering equal doses of pure Alaskan determination that might roll over her and a heart laid bare, overflowing with the deepest concern.

Cobie choked back some tears, then stepped forward. She pressed a hand against his cheek. The touch seared him. It was all he could do not to flinch under the heat of it.

"Okay, Adam, okay." Then Cobie did something completely unexpected. She stepped closer and stood on her toes until her face was near Adam's. And she just held it there, with her eyes closed, her breaths coming fast, as if she struggled with those tears she wouldn't shed. "I hear everything you said, and maybe some things you didn't."

Adam didn't think she wanted a kiss. No, this was something more—a need that he feared he could never fill. But somehow, someway, she seemed to be drawing strength from him. And maybe she didn't want a kiss, but her nearness drove him insane. One thing he knew, he and Cobie had a connection he could never explain.

She stepped back, flustered, and opened her eyes.

Adam cleared his throat. "Let me walk you out, then."

She didn't look at him again as he followed her out the door. She paused to lock it from the outside. He would walk her out, and then he'd ask if he could see her home, make sure the house was empty and safe. Take this one moment at a time.

Lights illuminated the parking lot, which was empty except for their two vehicles, which sat side by side, but Main Street was still busy at this hour. People heading home from work, coming or going to dinner somewhere. Cobie and Adam walked in silence. He wanted to ask if she'd heard anything about her father or about the investigation—because he hadn't gotten anything out of the police or Ray— but after their conversation in her office, he wasn't sure he could get back to normal just yet.

A concussive explosion blew up the night.

The force slammed into his body, lifting him into the air, whooshing him forward until he landed on the concrete. Debris rained down, splattering the pavement around him, clanking against vehicles. Pain coursed through his body, and his ears rang. Stunned, he lay there far too long before shaking off the stupor.

What just happened?

Cobie...

Adam scrambled to his feet, dizziness knocking him into his vehicle. "Cobie..."

Flames burst from the building behind them and reached for the sky, sending shadows dancing around him. *Cobie.* He had to find Cobie. *God, please let her be safe, unharmed.*

His vision blurred, and he stumbled forward, then onto his knees. Spotting her limp form a few feet from him, he crawled over.

"No, Cobie." Sorrow sliced through his being as his heart hammered wildly.

Adam barely heard the fire truck sirens, barely registered emergency crews were on their way, as he looked for a serious injury. Prayed the force of the explosion hadn't wounded her internally.

Please, just be unconscious. Just be okay.

He wasn't sure where or how to touch her, to hold her. He didn't want to hurt her. As a member of the search and rescue team, he knew enough emergency first aid and should know what to do here. He automatically detached himself emotionally to get the job done with others. But this was Cobie. He wasn't sure if the blast had turned his brain to mush, or his emotions clouded his thoughts, but with Cobie lying there, he couldn't think straight.

Nearly overcome, his vision blurred again. He had to get past this. Shove through it, for her sake.

He found a pulse.

She was alive.

Hope surged through him, along with adrenaline.

Carefully, he lifted her, bringing her to him, cradling her against him, his heart breaking. He glanced up at the clear sky, the threat of more rain clouds in the distance, creeping over a crescent moon, but he couldn't see stars for the flames behind him—and for the tears blurring his eyes. Too much pain and grief. This was why he'd wanted to leave the memories behind.

Praying silently, he begged God for Cobie's life, much like he'd begged for her brother's life. His prayers hadn't worked before, but he wouldn't quit.

He could never quit.

The trucks arrived. Adam held her tighter, squeezed his eyes shut, feeling as if his own life were bleeding right out of him. Paramedics pulled her away, reassured him, though he still couldn't make out their words. They tried to check him over, ask where he was hurt, but his only concern was for Cobie. His thoughts were still unclear, his limbs shaking. The EMTs placed Cobie on a gurney and took her away from him. He should follow, but he didn't think he could walk. One of the EMTs looked Adam over, then tried to strap him into a gurney, too, but Adam wouldn't have it. He wanted to go with Cobie, but he could see he'd only get in their way. Somehow, he would get to the hospital, follow the ambulance.

Adam searched for his keys.

Leaning against his vehicle, he saw it. A chunk of siding and Sheetrock had landed on Cobie's windshield.

Oh, man... That could have landed on him or Cobie. They were fortunate.

He pressed the heels of his palms against his eyes. Fear roiled inside for Cobie. For what this could mean for her life once she recovered. And she had to recover; he couldn't let himself think any other way.

Police, firemen and emergency vehicles filled the parking lot, and yet Adam felt as if he stood alone, watching the flames engulf Cobie's pride and joy. He understood the feeling of building something that was your own, making it grow and blossom. The sense of achievement. He also understood how it felt to watch the business you built burn to the ground.

Déjà vu.

Pain of a different kind rocked through him.

It hadn't been two months since he'd watched his own business burn thanks to a pyromaniac gang member after Tracy Murray, soon to be wed to David, his fireman brother. But the man running the shots, taunting Tracy and her friends and family, had died in a fire of his own making. So this couldn't be him.

No, this had to be the work of another crazed maniac.

Adam let his gaze sweep the crowd and then drift off to the shadows creeping in the woods that hedged the office complex. Why had Cobie's office blown up? Was this the second attempt on her life?

And the question that had haunted him for days now—why would anyone want her dead?

Flashing lights filtered through the darkness. Her body ached; pounding seized her head. Cobie blinked her eyes open.

A face filled her vision, but chaos ensued in her periphery.

"What happened?" Her mind was numb, groggy, and she couldn't comprehend the answer given. Nor could she hear it. "What happened?" This time she yelled, and that cost her.

Unbearable pain seared through her head.

The man she now recognized as an EMT reassured her, pressed her back down on the gurney.

"Adam? There was a man with me, Adam Warren…" Her tongue was thick; her words slurred.

If only she could read the EMT's lips.

"Adam Warren? Where is he? Is he all right?" She tried to climb off the gurney. But she didn't get very far. Her limbs wouldn't cooperate any more than her brain.

Blackness edged her vision, but she fought it. She had to know that he was okay. Was he in another ambulance on the way to the hospital? With everything in her, Cobie yelled his name.

"Adam!" At least she thought she'd yelled. She could hear her voice inside her head, but that was all she could hear above the ringing.

Someone took her hand.

She turned her head. Then she saw the face she'd been looking for.

Adam.

He looked down on her, anguish edged across his features along with cuts and bruises and swelling. Dirt and grime. Her heart tripped in relief. Hot, salty moisture slid from her eyes down the sides of her face.

Despite his dirty, roughed-up face, he looked so handsome to her just then—his scruffy jaw and tangle of hair, even with a few sticks and debris hanging out of it. The cutest guy she'd ever seen. Her emotions were raw and vulnerable, and she found it impossible to shove aside the feelings surfacing. They were memories only, and they had no place in her life now.

Still… Cobie tried to push herself up on her elbows. "Adam." She didn't know what she would do if something had happened to him. "What happened?"

When he frowned, she turned her eyes to the flames the firemen were fighting. David Warren, one of Adam's brothers, was probably among the firefighters. In fact, it looked as though the entire Warren clan had arrived. Must have rushed to the scene when they learned Adam was involved. Cobie didn't have family—a support system—like that.

It made her sick. Made her jealous. Poured salt on her wounds.

The EMT started lifting the gurney into the ambulance.

"No, I don't want to go. I'm okay—I'm okay."

Adam shook his head almost violently. Grabbed her hand, leaned in close. "You were knocked out. The explosion… It was bad. This is just a precaution. I promise I'll meet you up there. You're not alone."

It seemed as if he was yelling at her, but she could barely make out his words. Though they came to her across a great abyss, they meant everything. They were life to her. A small piece of the ice around her heart melted—there was one person in the world who cared.

And Cobie knew that person was Adam.

You're not alone.

Despite all that was between them, he cared. She didn't know if that was a good thing or a bad thing. But her mind and body were too shell-shocked to push him away. He'd been her first thought when she'd come to.

The explosion.

Her mind finally wrapped around the meaning. Everything registered, knocking the breath from her again. This time, Cobie sat up on her elbows just as the EMT shoved her inside, though they hadn't shut the ambulance doors yet.

Her business. Her life. All that she'd worked for was up in flames now. She couldn't believe it was an accident. Someone was trying to kill her, but why? If they hadn't wanted the journal, then what were they after?

What was happening to her carefully constructed, safe and secure world?

TEN

In the small hospital clinic, Cobie rested on a bed behind a curtain, waiting on Shana to return with pain medication. Doc Harland's wife and clinic nurse was three decades younger than her husband, and both were Cobie's clients. Doc Harland, warm and jovial with his paunch, balding head and full healthy smile—with two crowns on the left bottom—told her she'd been lucky and only had a few bruises. A mild concussion, too. She didn't think she needed a doctor to tell her any of that, but it was good to know she didn't have any internal injuries. Her hearing would come back fully within a few days.

In the meantime, Chief Winters, flanked by Officer Stratford, had been in to ask her questions. They left without answers because she had none.

She pressed her hands over her face, holding the tears in, steadying her heart. Her business had been destroyed. She was just thankful none of her employees had been there. What was she going to do?

If people couldn't come to her, they'd have to go to the only other dentist in town, and they might not come back to her. How soon would she be able to rebuild? Get new equipment? Would the insurance pay, and how long would that take them? Too much to think about. It made her head hurt all the more.

The only positive was that she didn't have to stay in the clinic overnight for observation. Doc Harland would release her to Katy Warren. He didn't want her staying alone in case she needed anything— but she had a feeling more was going on behind the scenes. Adam and the good doctor and Katy were working against her. Well, okay, *for* her, in their well-meaning way.

Shana came back and handed her printed prescriptions signed by the doctor. "Now, Doc says you're to wait here until someone arrives to drive you home. Do you know who'll be coming for you?"

Adam had told her he would come, and that she wasn't alone. But he wasn't here yet. Was she wrong to count on him to be there for her like he'd said? Counting on someone else, having expectations, had always been a big mistake for her, leaving her empty and wounded. Hadn't she learned that from her experience with her father?

Adam probably decided she wasn't worth the energy. Being with her was certainly a dangerous endeavor. She could move on and forget about him. She could and she would.

But she'd agreed to stay at Katy's in order to get out of here. Should she head to Katy's like Doc Harland believed, or just go home?

"No, I can drive—"

Then it hit her. Her Explorer was still in the parking lot. Had it been damaged during the explosion? Anger and frustration knotted in her throat. Cobie couldn't finish the sentence. Shana stared at her, sympathy written all over her face and in her beautiful smile. She had shiny, unnaturally white teeth, but that's what she'd wanted and Cobie had obliged.

"I'm here!" The curtain jerked open. Breathless, Adam stood there. "I'm here." He lowered his voice to a hospital-quiet pitch.

"Adam," she said. Why'd he have to show up? She'd already tucked thoughts of him safe and sound in the vault that she'd decided never to open again. "What are you doing here?"

Rude. She had to be rude to hide her completely traitorous relief at seeing him.

"I told you I'd be here. Sorry for the delay."

Shana smiled at Adam. "Hey, Adam. I think the good dentist here could use a ride." She winked and left them alone.

Cobie opened her mouth. Then shut it promptly. What could she say to that?

"That's why I'm here. Well, part of the reason." Adam came closer and took her hand in his, sending a warm current up her arm. That spark. That stupid spark. She remembered the first time she'd felt that with him. They were just kids, teenagers. But why did she have to feel it again? Feel it now? She didn't want any sparks with Adam. Too much stood between them.

"What's the other part of the reason?" Cobie tugged her hand free, tucked it away beneath her arm.

"To see if you're okay." His brow furrowed. "You could have been killed today."

"You, too." Her prescriptions in hand, Cobie stood. Oh, wow, did she feel that. There wasn't a place on her body that didn't ache, but her head overshadowed it all.

"Take it easy—take it slow." Adam gripped her arms.

"What about you? Aren't you in pain?" She regretted the tone she'd taken, but why did it seem as though he'd weathered this much better than she had?

"Yes, I'm in pain. But I don't have a concussion."

"How do you not have a concussion?" She pressed a finger to her aching temple. "Forget I asked that. I don't even know what I'm saying. I need to get out of here."

"Good idea."

"I'd appreciate a ride, Adam, since my… How is my Explorer? Did you happen to see?"

"There might be a few dings on it." He picked

at something in her hair, then brushed his hand through it. "Mine is more drivable than yours right now, let's just say."

She pursed her lips. "Oh."

What would happen next? What was *left* to happen next? She held her tongue, tried to stay calm. Anger made her head pound all the more.

"David says they won't officially know the cause of the explosion for a few days, but unofficially they found evidence." Adam backed away and ran a hand over his face. "Let's get out of here."

"Evidence, Adam?"

He held her elbow and ushered her through the curtain.

"You can't leave me hanging!" Cobie winced when she noticed that her volume had brought a few looks. Clinic staff, people waiting to see the doctor—a mom with her daughter, an elderly man, and a couple of hikers, one with what looked like a twisted ankle. Her head hammered on top of it all.

Adam assisted her out the door.

"Evidence of what?" This time she lowered her voice. Of course, now there was no one near to hear them, so it didn't matter. As they stepped into the night, she tugged her arm free. Adam leaned close, and Cobie eyed him at an angle.

His jaw twitched. "An explosive device."

"An explosive device?"

"A bomb, Cobie. They found evidence of a bomb."

* * *

Adam drove her back to his grandmother's in silence broken only by the rhythmic slide of the windshield wipers. The clouds had finally moved in, bringing the usual rain with them. This was certainly not the way he'd wanted Cobie convinced she shouldn't stay at her house and that she should come back to his grandmother's. His last words before they climbed into his truck—dinged and roughened by the explosion but running—echoed through his head. Probably hers, too.

A bomb.

Twice this week, he'd almost lost her. He wasn't going anywhere until whoever was terrorizing her was behind bars. He would get his things and stay in the garage apartment at Grandma Katy's. But he wouldn't tell Cobie about that yet. Didn't want to scare her off.

She stared out the window into the night. Had she noticed he took the long way around so he wouldn't pass the building that had housed her dental practice? He didn't want her to have to watch her business smolder, look at the devastation, breathe in the stench of all her hard labor reduced to ashes. Nor did she ask him to take her there, even to see her vehicle.

It would all be there tomorrow.

And it was beyond surreal, bringing back the complete devastation he'd felt the day his bicycle shop had burned to the ground. He'd moved on, or was trying to, but now he was back in it with Cobie. He felt as devastated now over her business as he had his own.

She groaned a little. Shifted in the seat and let out a breath. Probably thinking things through. He should say something. But he didn't know what to say. Any words would only come across sounding like empty platitudes.

At least he knew she'd be safe tonight. But how could he keep her safe going forward?

Who had planted the bomb? Tried to strangle her? Broken into her home? And what had happened to her father? Had he been murdered? Adam wouldn't be able to sleep for thinking someone might try again.

At least if she stayed at his grandmother's there was a good chance that whoever was after her wouldn't know where she was. They'd have to ferret her out, and that would take some extra time and effort. And Chief Winters had to see the need for the police to watch over the house. This new incident bumped everything up to an even more serious level. He hadn't shared it with Cobie yet, but David had mentioned that Chief Winters said he would try to stop by later to talk to her more about everything that had happened.

He pulled into the driveway, uncomfortable with all the cars parked at his grandmother's house.

Seemed everyone was here tonight. What had he expected? They would want to make sure Cobie was all right. And check on Adam.

Doubting she wanted to face all his siblings and their growing families, he frowned as he glanced at Cobie. She sat there looking cold and numb. Shell-shocked. That's all it was. She was shocked. Who could blame her? Someone had tried to kill her twice, and add that to finding her father's body.

How much more could she take?

Adam wished he knew what he could say, but there were no words. So he reached across the cab, laid his hand over hers. "I'm sorry."

She didn't shift or move her hand away, only stared out the window. Looked as if a few snow flurries mixed in with the rain. They were small, inconsequential. It was too early for anything more.

"I was sorry to hear that your business burned," she said. "I felt sick for you. I should have sent a card. Something."

"I understand why you didn't." She'd wanted to forget she knew him.

"No. That's inexcusable. I should have done… something. But I didn't know then how it felt, losing everything like that."

He knew not to point out that after the fire he still had his family, which was more than he could say for Cobie.

"I know that you understand what I'm going

through now. You can understand that better than anyone."

"There's a big difference between the two incidents, between my business burning and yours. Nobody broke into my home. Nobody is trying to kill me." Yet could he really be sure that the bomb was meant to kill Cobie? It had gone off after hours, when she shouldn't have been inside.

She turned her face to him, her big blue eyes latching on to something inside him. "And yet you almost died today, too."

ELEVEN

A couple of days later, Cobie woke early to the alarm on her cell. She considered cutting herself a break and sleeping in yet again. Doing what Doc had ordered and rest. Let Katy take care of her. But she'd already given herself an extra day to lie there numb and foggy, and all that accomplished was giving her mind time to go crazy thinking about everything that had happened. Well, she was done resting. Done with doing nothing at all. Time for action.

She instinctively grabbed the pain pills on the table next to the bed but then caught herself—she wouldn't take them today. She might not have a business to go to, and she'd have to make the necessary phone calls to deal with that, and she might not be ready to go home just yet, where she'd be alone and not a little scared, but she could try to meet with Dr. Burkov.

That was a goal, something to keep her mind and heart from drowning in a quagmire. A first step to being proactive in solving this. He hadn't returned her call that she knew of, but at least her laptop hadn't suffered any damage and she pulled it off the table, sat up in bed and opened it to access her emails. Dr. Burkov had responded to her email regarding his sympathy card, and he was eager to meet her, today if possible.

Today? She groaned, but she'd wanted to take action.

In defiance of her aching, bruised body, she rose from the soft warm bed, compliments of Katy Warren. While she showered and dressed, she thought things through, though stringing coherent thoughts together took precious energy. If someone had killed her father and now wanted to kill her, Cobie had better find out who it was. She'd start with why.

The night of the explosion she'd answered Chief Winters's questions while all the Warren siblings hovered somewhere in the house. Their presence had made her uncomfortable, but it was better than going to the station. To his credit, Chief Winters was concerned for her safety and said his department would find the criminals, with all due diligence, working with the state police and Forest Service LEI, as well. From what she knew about him, he was a good man. But that was part of the problem. He was only a man; all the police were only human. Fallible, imperfect. She had no doubt they would do their best, but sometimes that wasn't enough.

She recalled what had happened to Tracy Murray. How many attempts had been made on her life before the perpetrator was caught. Knowing that helped spur Cobie on. Encouraged her that she couldn't just wait around for the police to figure things out. She could die while she waited. She had to take steps to find out who wanted her dead. And along the way, she had a feeling she would find out what happened to her father, too.

His death was somehow tied to this. She knew it.

On her way down, Cobie met Katy heading up the stairs to check on her. Cobie assured her she was fine, but she had some business to take care of. Katy wasn't happy about her leaving, but there wasn't much she could do. Fortunately for Cobie, Adam had agreed to head out on a search and rescue for two hikers, promising to return soon, so he wasn't present to talk her out of going or insist on going with her. Cobie was glad to hear that he was getting back into his Mountain Cove life. She still felt guilty that he'd changed his travel plans because of her. Today was the day he'd arranged to leave.

On the one hand, she felt bad about messing up his plans. At the same time she was grateful to have someone, a friend like him, on her side. She called a cab service to take her to the floatplane dock and thought about how she was leaving that friend behind to meet with Dr. Burkov. But the man was harmless, a longtime friend of her father's, and

Cobie wanted to know what he would tell her that he might not say with a stranger present.

Billy wasn't available, but another pilot was there preparing to deliver packages to an island and agreed to fly her to Juneau. Two hours later, Cobie stood across the street from the museum and stared at the coffee shop next door where she was to meet Dr. Burkov. She'd looked him up on the internet to find out more than she already knew. He'd gotten his PhD in New Mexico and had been part of excavations in Alaska, Arizona, South America and Russia. He'd also been curator for a museum, but now he taught various courses at the university in Juneau, where he'd been for fifteen years at least. He'd accomplished a lot for his age.

She wondered if he was already at the coffee shop, waiting on her.

Here goes something or nothing.

Wrapped in her raincoat, she held her umbrella up and crossed the street, hoping she'd recognize him from his picture on the university website. She'd been a child when she'd last seen him in person. Cobie entered the café, briefcase with her laptop at her side, and glanced around as she closed up her umbrella. *There.* Far corner of the shop, his attention on his tablet device. In his late fifties, his face was grayish, with thin lips and eyebrows, a protruding nose and a serious expression, all confirming his Russian descent to go with his name.

She strolled around the tables and through the patron-filled shop. He didn't glance up until she was almost on him.

His cell resting on the table suddenly vibrated, a man's image flashing on the screen. Dr. Burkov frowned and slid the phone into his pocket without answering. When he looked up at Cobie, he smiled and stood, offering his hand. She took it, and he wrapped her hand in both of his, filling her with warmth and jarring a positive memory or two of her father's friend and colleague from years before.

Compassion and sympathy filled his eyes. "Now I can offer my condolences in person. I'm so sorry for your loss, Cobie."

He gestured for her to take a seat across from him, which she did. She shrugged off her raincoat and let it hang over the chair, then ordered coffee and a scone when the waitress appeared.

"Thank you for agreeing to meet me on such short notice, Dr. Burkov," she said.

"Please, it's Yuri. And think nothing of it. As I said in my email, I can't tell you how sorry I am for your loss. He'll be missed." Yuri lifted his mug and drank, eyeing her over the rim.

His gray eyes were sharp, and filled with an odd mix of grief, compassion and curiosity. He had his own questions. What did he want to know from her?

"He'll be missed? Why do you say that?" The

waitress brought Cobie's coffee and cream, and Cobie thanked her without taking her eyes off Yuri.

He set his cup down, leaned back in his chair and studied her. "We've been friends a long time. Colleagues a long time. Why wouldn't I miss him?"

"I didn't mean to offend you—that wasn't my intention," she said. "I'd like to know when the last time you saw him was. That's all. For myself, I haven't seen him in years."

"Ah. I understand you better, then. Let me reassure you, I haven't seen him in years, either. But we've had conversations on the phone or via email. He'd often share about his work, knowing that I would welcome lively intellectual conversation about the subjects we both loved. But though I hadn't wanted to mention this, he contacted me some months ago. He'd been…let go, shall we say, from his project and was looking for a new one."

Hurt cut through her. This wasn't how she'd meant for the conversation to go. She hadn't been prepared for how it would feel to know that her father had contacted this man more frequently than he had her. Yuri probably knew her father better than she did. He knew about the projects he'd worked on.

But fired? Yuri was lying. She wouldn't believe it. Her mouth grew parched. "What was the project?"

"A shipwreck. He was the archaeologist on contract with Deep Water Marine Salvage. You could say he was the go-between for the state. The information he provided would help them decide what they could keep for the museum or what went to the salvage company."

Her father had an extensive education that included underwater archaeology. She knew exploring a shipwreck had been one of his dreams. All the more reason to believe he hadn't been fired—he'd have been very motivated to do his best work.

"Tell me more about the shipwreck."

He frowned, looked at his mug, then met her gaze. "A gold rush era shipwreck, here in the Inside Passage. The SS *Bateman*, a luxury steamer traveling from Skagway to British Columbia in 1905. The passengers were wealthy, and, in addition to any valuables they might have stored on board, the steam supposedly carried a cargo of gold bullion. At the time, it was valued at eight million dollars."

"Supposedly?"

"There have been many salvage attempts over the decades, over the century, in fact, but none have recovered the gold. It's almost become legendary. Mythical."

"And that's what my father was helping to find?"

"Yes, if it exists, along with other valuables."

Cobie let the information sink in. What would the gold be worth today? Murder would be a small price to pay. Now Cobie would get to her real reason for coming to see Yuri.

"How did you know he was dead? How did you know to send the sympathy card?"

Something Cobie couldn't read flashed in his eyes. Something that made her skin crawl.

He released a half laugh along with his smile. Leaned forward and drank more coffee. "Yes, now I see how that might have looked to you when you opened it. I have a friend in the Forest Service who knew of my affiliation with your father and thought I would want to know. After all, much of our fieldwork we do in conjunction with the Forest Service and the like."

Cobie knew her features had hardened, and she put on a smile she didn't feel. "Of course, that makes sense. Did your friend share any of the details?"

Yuri lifted a thin brow. "I'm afraid not. Would I be insensitive to ask how he died?"

What did it matter? He'd asked the question anyway. "I don't know how he died. I found his body in a cave. The police are investigating. We won't know, officially, for a while longer if he died of natural causes or if he was murdered." Though Cobie already had her own strong suspicions.

"That's troubling news."

They sat in silence. He studied the table, studied Cobie as if measuring her, deciding if he could share more with her. She did the same. Should she share with him everything that had happened? Could she trust him now that she believed he was lying about her father's termination? She couldn't know for certain, though, and likely her own emotions and biases colored her opinion.

Still, Cobie thought she should leave, and she moved to do so. But Yuri started in, sharing stories about her father in an obvious attempt to lighten the conversation and lift Cobie's spirits. And hadn't she wanted those stories? She half listened, half thought about what to do next.

When the conversation died again, and the afternoon grew late, Cobie knew it was time to leave. "Thank you, Yuri, for meeting me. For spending almost an entire afternoon with me. I'm sure I've taken enough of your time, and I need to get back to Mountain Cove." She stood and gathered her umbrella and briefcase.

"If there's anything else I can do, please let me know. I'll deliver you back to the airport, of course. No need to call a cab."

That would give her one last opportunity to ask questions, anything else that came to mind. Or for him to share. She hadn't been able to shake the sense that he knew something he wasn't telling her. Once inside his vehicle, classical music piped through the speakers, and he turned it down.

"Cobie, if you hear something more about how your father died, please let me know. Maybe I can be of assistance. It sounds to me as if you're trying to find the missing pieces to the mystery of his death. I'm concerned about your safety, frankly. Does anyone else know that you came to see me?"

"Of course they do," Cobie lied. She wasn't about to tell him the truth. She suddenly realized that she shouldn't have come to meet him alone. She couldn't trust anyone.

Not even Dr. Burkov.

"I'm glad to hear it. While you're here, I think I have something that might interest you."

"What is it?"

"I'll have to show you. It's at my house."

A memory flashed in her mind. Her father was on the phone talking to Yuri about his private collection. Her father didn't seem happy about that. Maybe Yuri planned to show her the collection. The coffee shop was one thing; to be alone with him at his house wasn't a good idea. "I'm afraid I'll miss my flight."

"It won't delay you at all."

Her skin tingled and crawled, and Cobie was ready to flee this ride.

"I don't know, Dr. Burkov...er... Yuri. Maybe you can show me on my next trip. Can you at least tell me what it is?"

Yuri remained silent. Cobie noticed the vehicle accelerated as he steered up the mountain, taking the curves too quickly. His sedan veered much too close to a rocky sea cliff, reminding her of her jump into oblivion mere days ago. Yuri didn't know about that, but still, his driving was reckless. What was the matter with him?

"You're scaring me. Could you please slow down?"

"My apologies. Sometimes I get lost in thought. Carried away. I'm accustomed to this drive, so it doesn't bother me so much. Now, what was your question again?"

Cobie regretted that she'd gotten into the vehicle with the man in the first place. "I told you that I won't have time to go to your house today, so please take me to the airport like you initially offered. I'm happy to hear about whatever it is you want to show me, then see it on my next trip here."

Approaching a four-way stoplight, Yuri slowed the sedan. Cobie decided this was her chance. She might not get another. A small but busy mom-and-pop gas station and convenience store stood at the corner.

When the vehicle stopped, she quickly unlocked and opened the door in one fluid motion. Yuri didn't have the chance to protest or prevent her from getting away—or cause her any harm, if that had been his intention. Pulse pounding in her ears, blocking out all other sounds, she stepped out and drew in a breath of freedom, then leaned into the vehicle.

"Thanks for the offer. But right now I need some fresh air. Maybe some other time, okay?"

She shut the door and hurried out of the street

and onto the sidewalk, next to businesses and people. Lots of people. She needed to disappear in the store. From there she would call a cab. She might never know what he would have shown her, but she'd been an idiot to come here alone. It was much too dangerous.

Other than Adam and his family, she didn't know whom she could trust.

He thought they'd come to at least some sort of agreement that he was in this for the long haul. And so even though it wasn't technically any of his business, Adam fumed as he paced Cobie's porch, waiting on her to answer the door. After he'd come back from a SAR mission much later than he'd intended, his grandmother had told him Cobie had moved home, and she'd done that knowing even Doc wanted her at Katy's. Chief Winters had instructed his officers to drive by Grandma Katy's place, keep a watch on the house, and Adam had moved into the garage. But what did any of that matter if Cobie was back at her house now?

His grandmother also explained that Cobie had flown to Juneau and back today.

It wasn't his business, but he couldn't stand on the sidelines and watch someone hurt Cobie. Kill her. Bad enough he'd been involved in her brother's death.

He'd thought they were pushing past all that to get

through this crisis, at the very least. He'd thought she *needed* him. If he was honest with himself, he was as hurt as he was angry.

The door cracked open, and she peered out at him. Then she swung it wide. She turned and walked into the house without as much as a hello, apparently expecting him to follow. He drew in a breath, preparing to speak his mind.

"I know why you're here, and you don't have to worry. A security guy's coming in an hour to install a top-of-the-line system." She busied herself in the kitchen, finishing off a pasta creation, despite the mess that remained inside the house. She poured a couple of glasses of iced tea and offered him one.

Her words deflated him, ruined his spiel. He took the tea. "You didn't have to do that, you know. Move out. You could have stayed until this was over. I had moved into the garage apartment to help keep you safe. Was going to tell you today when I got home. All the same, you could have shared your plans with those of us who are worried about you."

She stopped what she was doing over the stove, those big blue eyes of hers taking him in before she returned to stirring the pasta. "I don't want to disrupt your life any more than I already have. You missed your flight out of here. You had big plans, Adam."

He set the glass on the counter too hard. "I don't

care about that anymore. What's it going to take for you to understand I'm not going away?"

Adam moved around the counter and into the kitchen. Pressed his hands on her shoulders, let them slide down her arms. "I know you haven't forgotten what we went through before. That you blame me. But don't shut me out now. After this is over, you can go back to blaming me for Brad's death. But I'm part of this. I was there almost the moment it started. I won't let you go through this alone."

He tried to hold her gaze, hoping she'd see everything in his eyes, but she looked away and turned back to the stove. "The police found no prints or anything they could use from the break-in. If it weren't for what I learned today from Yuri—"

"Wait. Who?"

"Dr. Burkov. A colleague of my father's. I found a sympathy card from him. He'd sent it to my office, and it arrived the day my office blew up. I thought it was strange that he knew of my father's death already. I want to know what's going on, and I thought he was a good place to start. So I went to Juneau to meet him for coffee."

"You should have told me. I could have gone with you. You have no idea who you can trust, Cobie."

"You're right. I won't argue with you. I don't know who I can trust."

She went back to scooping her pasta into bowls,

then handed him one, obviously assuming he'd eat. She was right. They slid into chairs at the kitchen table, thanked the Lord for the food and ate in silence.

"Cobie, what else happened today? What did you find out from Dr. Burkov?" Adam fought to keep his tone even, but he was more than furious. Again, not his right. She could refuse his help if he pushed too far. But he didn't want her looking for answers alone.

And that's why she'd done it. She thought she was alone. How did he convince her that she wasn't?

"Dr. Burkov said my father was let go, in effect fired, from a project. A shipwreck in the Inside Passage, one of the old gold rush ships. Something doesn't sound right to me. My father was all about his work, and he was highly valued for that. He wouldn't have been easy to replace, so why would they fire him?"

Adam wondered if she was considering digging further, but she said nothing. The way she pursed her lips, Adam had the feeling there was much more. "Cobie, what *aren't* you telling me?"

She squared her shoulders and measured her words. "Then Yuri offered to give me a ride to the airport, but when I got into the car, he said he wanted to take me to his house to show me something."

Adam's spine stiffened. He didn't like the sound

of that. He stopped eating, put down his fork and leaned back. "Tell me."

"I don't know what he wanted to show me. I got out of his vehicle when he was stopped at a red light."

Adam couldn't help his grin despite the seriousness of the situation. Despite his concern for her safety. "I guess you showed him."

She huffed, then focused on her food again.

They continued to eat in silence. Adam was glad to see she had an appetite. He decided he wouldn't interrupt her with more questions. He'd give her the space she needed to process the day and tell him everything.

"I got a weird vibe about the whole thing. I think he knew something he wasn't telling me. He might have told me if I had gone with him to his house, but I wasn't willing to do that. I shouldn't have gone to see him alone. But he was a friend of my father's. Had sent a card. They'd known each other for years. I didn't think meeting him at a coffee shop would be a problem. But I won't make that mistake twice."

She set her fork down, tossed her napkin into the pasta bowl.

"I'm glad to hear that." Adam stood from his chair and moved to Cobie. He pulled her to stand and dragged her to the fireplace to stand in front of the mantel, let the heat chase away the chill. There was no place to sit other than at the dining table since the ruins of her sofa and chairs had been carted away and she hadn't replaced them yet. "So take me with you next time. You're not alone in this. I won't let you be, even if you want to be. Take me with you. We'll figure this out together." He thought they'd already been over this, but apparently Cobie would take some more convincing. Still, he could tell she'd been processing everything, and maybe she'd needed the day alone to do that.

She shrugged. "I probably shouldn't say this, but it feels good that someone cares. I keep thinking about my father and how he died alone in that cave."

Definitely processing. Now they were getting somewhere.

Adam thought he heard her loud and clear. She didn't want to die alone. Neither did he, but hopefully neither of them would have to worry about that anytime soon. Except with the attempt on her life, longevity was a definite concern.

Then she was in his arms again. Just like the first time, he didn't know how it happened. Had he pulled her to him? Or had some instinctive magnetic force pulled them together? He went with the natural flow of things and wrapped his arms around her, willing her to understand that he was here with her. Would see her through it, as unlikely a pair as they were with the past they shared.

Cobie nestled against him. For this moment in time, Adam considered that maybe they were being given a chance to start over. Their relationship was like a phoenix of sorts. It had burned down before, but maybe they could both start fresh in every aspect and build something new out of the ashes. But when she pulled away, he saw in her eyes what he hadn't wanted to see.

She still blamed him for her brother's death. She would never forget that, and neither would he. They would never get a second chance.

TWELVE

Her father had died alone, and it broke her heart to think of it. Looking at Adam now, she knew one thing… *God, I don't want to die alone.*

In the meantime, she didn't want to live alone, either. And the worst of it? There could be no remedy for that kind of loneliness—she could never be with the one man she'd ever wanted. She'd been hurt, devastated by the two men in her life she'd loved—her father and Adam. Being alone was safer. It would protect her from ever getting hurt that way again. Maybe in the end, the loneliness would make her numb to the pain of it. That's what her father had done. He'd thrown himself into his work. She didn't like the sound of that—that she could be weak like her father, ignore the possibility of love and relationships around her to avoid the hurt. But she didn't know what else to do.

Except she had to find out what happened to him, before it happened to her.

When Adam ran a finger down her cheek, she realized she'd been caught up and stepped away. "I'm going there, Adam. To the shipwreck."

"Why would you do that?"

"Because it was the last place he worked. Plus, the island where we found his body isn't that far from the shipwreck." Over the last century there'd been several salvage attempts, so she'd found plenty of information on the internet. "Don't you think there could be a connection?"

"Then let's tell the police. Tell Ray. Let them work it out."

"Don't worry. I'll talk to Chief Winters. Send him an email about today. In case something happens, I don't want any information, any clues or details, to be lost."

Adam frowned. "Nothing is going to happen to you, Cobie. I won't let it. The next place you go, I'm going with you. But don't you think it's best to just let him do his job? Let him figure this out?"

"My father's death isn't his priority. Isn't even his jurisdiction. And while my safety might be a high priority, the two are tied together. I want to be proactive, not just sit around and wait for the next attempt on my life."

"Your father's death is *Ray's* priority, along with the state police—that is, if the ME finds that his death was suspicious aside from how we found him. Why don't you email Ray about this shipwreck information, too?"

"Okay. Sure. And then what? I guess you just want me to sit around and wait for someone to try to kill me again."

Adam looked hurt. He started clearing the dishes. She realized he had no intention of leaving for a while yet. So much for a quiet evening at home—her first in several nights—to think things through and tackle the mess on her hands. She glanced at the clock on the wall. When was Dana's husband supposed to get there? He installed security systems, and, given her current predicament, he had insisted on coming out this evening to install a top-of-the-line system for her.

Cobie joined Adam in the kitchen to stack dishes in the sink. A warm, fuzzy feeling washed over her. In a perfect world—a world where her brother and father were both still alive, and maybe even her mother had survived her birth—she and Adam might be in a relationship. Dating, engaged or even married. In a perfect world, that felt right and good, and she allowed, just for a moment, that feeling, that dream, to wash over her and wrap her up.

If only she could have that instead of this, this broken life she couldn't begin to fix.

Adam turned to face her. He ran his palms down her arms. They'd gotten awfully cozy, it seemed, since their lives had collided once again. And though she had plenty of reasons to push him away, she couldn't bring herself to do it.

"I don't think he's going to want you…or us…to investigate. But let's say we decide to do this, go to the shipwreck, how do we make that happen? These salvage sites can be highly sensitive, confidential. You can't just show up there and expect them to be willing to talk to you. So what's the plan?"

Cobie proceeded to load the dishwasher while Adam helped. "I thought I'd call the state archaeologist. My father would have known him. Tell him that my father is dead, if he doesn't already know, and maybe talk him into giving me a name for a contact at the salvage company. I'll say that I want to see what my father worked on last, just as a way to connect to him."

"You think he'll go for that?"

"It's worth a try." She closed the dishwasher and started the cycle.

"When is this security guy supposed to show up? I don't want you to be alone until your house is secure."

Exhausted, she wasn't sure she wanted anyone, even if it was her employee's husband, in her house for hours rigging things. And she was torn about Adam. Didn't want him to go yet. Didn't want him to stay.

"Let me call Dana—she's my receptionist. Her husband is the one installing the system." Cobie sagged at the thought that her employees might find other jobs before she could get back up and running. "I'll just grab my cell."

She went to the bedroom and spotted her purse on the dresser. Cobie pulled out the cell, then heard a noise outside. Cobie slid the side of the curtain back so she could see.

A face stared back at her from the window.

"Call 9-1-1 and stay here!" Adam ran outside with the flashlight after Cobie explained what she'd seen. Her scream had scared off the face in the window. That and her discovery.

From inside, Cobie flipped all the outside lights on, illuminating most of the yard. The corners and bushes provided dark shadows for someone to hide in. But Adam found no one. When he made sure whoever had been looking through the window was gone, he shined the flashlight into the woods across the street.

A police cruiser arrived with flashing lights. Behind it, Chief Winters himself drove up in his Jeep Cherokee just as Adam was about to cross the street and search the woods.

Chief Winters climbed out of his vehicle and approached Adam. "What happened?"

"Someone was outside looking in the window."

"You're sure it wasn't some kid, some Peeping Tom?"

"Of course it wasn't. Her curtains were drawn

for one thing. Maybe this guy was trying to find a way into her bedroom to search again."

"With you both inside the house?"

"We were having dinner. Had been in the dining room and kitchen a couple of hours. Maybe he thought he could get in and out of the bedroom without us noticing. But I think he escaped through the woods. I want to follow him, find him. This has to stop."

Chief Winters grabbed Adam's arm and swung him around toward the house. "Don't even think about it. Let's see what we can find outside the window, shoe prints and the like."

Beneath the bedroom window, they found the prints they were looking for. Terry took pictures while Adam shone the flashlight. "We'll come back tomorrow to see if we can find anything else in daylight."

Chief Winters had gone in the house to question Cobie, stating he wanted to see her alone, without Adam. He probably wouldn't want to be interrupted, but they had finished outside and Adam was done waiting. "Let's get inside."

A van pulled up. The security system guy had finally arrived, just in time. Adam wanted to laugh at that.

He greeted the guy—Tom Koontz—and led him in. Cobie sat on one of the dining chairs, talking to Chief Winters as he took notes. She looked as if she was still shaken. When she saw Tom, she rose and greeted him.

"Do you mind if I have a few minutes with him so he can get started on the system?" she asked.

Chief Winters nodded and moved to stand with Adam and Terry.

"What do you think?" Adam asked.

"She got a good look at him, so we'll need her at the station to look at some pictures to see if she can identify the suspect. If not, we'll get a sketch artist in. But I'll tell you I don't like this one bit, her living alone and someone harassing her like this. The attempts on her life."

"Are you any closer to figuring out why someone wants to hurt her? Did you read her email?"

"I read the email. There are several law enforcement entities working on this—Mountain Cove PD, the Alaska State Troopers, the Forest Service LEI. That's one problem. Coordinating and sharing of information about her father's death and about her attacker. The cases could be related, but I don't have the time to travel, or the manpower to investigate every leg of something that isn't in my jurisdiction. Something that isn't a priority for the other entities, especially since we don't know the cause of death yet. All I can do is trust the others to do their jobs with this one investigation out of hundreds on their plates. And then I can try to keep her safe. Catch this guy when he's in Mountain Cove and stop him."

Adam saw the futility of it in the Mountain Cove chief of police's eyes.

He watched Cobie talking to Tom and wished he was over there to make sure Tom understood how serious this was. But this conversation was important, too.

"What can I do?" he asked.

"I thought you were leaving town. Would be gone for months is the way I heard it."

"I was, sure, but with Cobie's situation… Look, I feel like I'm the only friend she's got." Maybe she had others, how would he know? He had been the only one with her tonight. And, frankly, he didn't trust another soul to see this through with her.

"Why don't you keep your travel plans and take her with you?"

Now there was an idea, except he'd canceled the flight and first leg of his plans. And anyway… "I don't think she'd agree to that."

"I see. Well, you asked what you could do. Try to convince her to get away from here. Maybe if she's gone for a while, we'll catch the person or persons responsible for her attacks. Maybe she'll even confide in you why someone would want to kill her. What they were looking for inside the house."

Cobie approached. "Chief Winters, I wonder if you could tell me when the medical examiner will release my father. I need to coordinate with Barbara Stemmons in Seattle to make funeral arrangements."

The chief rubbed his jaw. Acted as if he was measuring his words. "The ME is still waiting to ID the body, Cobie."

"What? I don't understand."

"You know, DNA. Dental records. He's still waiting on those."

Cobie looked confused. Adam guessed she didn't have her father's dental records. Their relationship had always been a mystery to him.

"I identified the body. I found the necklace that belonged to him." Her face grew pale. "The clothes…"

Adam imagined she didn't like to think of her father's decomposed body. That had been a hard thing to see. "Why does he need more?"

Chief Winters directed his words at Cobie. "In case it's not your father."

THIRTEEN

Even with a top-of-the-line security system, Cobie hadn't been able to fall asleep until the early hours of the morning. She kept seeing that face in her window. How could she ever get it out of her mind? The face—a man in his midthirties—had appeared as surprised to see her open the curtains and look out as she had been to see him. Had he believed he could simply climb through her window with her and Adam on the other side of the house?

What was so important? What did someone think she had? And why the attempts on her life if they were only looking for something?

After the police, Tom and then Adam finally left her alone, she should have felt safe in her home. The system was armed. No one could get inside without her knowing. But still she felt on edge. So what if her house had a security system? She couldn't stay inside forever, and she wasn't safe outside—even on some remote island. This had to stop.

Since it had been too late last night to call the

state archaeologist, she'd found his email on the website easily enough and sent him a message. Now, to see if he'd answered. Cobie tossed the covers off. Might as well make some coffee and get going. The sooner she found answers, the better. Correction, the sooner she and Adam found answers. She'd promised him she would include him, and so she would. It was foolish to do this alone. She would let the police know about what she found, too. They needed all the help they could get. But just like Chief Winters had explained to her last night, the police couldn't be everywhere all the time, and no one could know more about what was going on than she could. She had the feeling he thought she was keeping something from him, that she knew what this was all about.

God, why is someone trying to kill me? What do I have that they want?

While the coffee brewed, she booted up the laptop, hoping for an email from Miles Cooper, the state archaeologist. It was a long shot, but her father would likely have known the man, and hopefully he would recognize her name.

Coffee mug in hand, she drank in the strong brew. *Mmm. Just right.* That should get her going this morning. She opened up her email and scanned down the page.

Bingo. Miles Cooper had replied.

Her palms grew clammy. She sat down to open

the email and read. He expressed his sympathy and condolences for her loss and understood her need to visit the site where her father had worked and visit the salvage vessel—the *Voyager*. He promised to contact Deep Water Marine Salvage to look into getting her on the vessel, though he could make no promises. He'd been the one to sign off on the attempts to retrieve the gold, but he had only done so through pressure from government officials, meaning he had some pull with the salvage company.

Cobie closed the email. If there was one thing she knew, it was that archaeologists didn't like treasure hunters—they often destroyed history in the process and prevented artifacts from being shared with the world. If the state had signed off on this effort, then the highest archaeological standards would be upheld. Gold valuing in the millions of dollars would bring on pressure to retrieve it.

And maybe even pressure to kill someone.

After checking the rest of her emails, she dressed for the day, then called her insurance company again. No progress could be made until the investigation of the explosion was complete. And depending on those results, she might be able to rebuild, but she couldn't collect insurance on the loss of income while she rebuilt because of the terrorism exclusion clause. Meanwhile, she was still waiting to hear back on her car insurance. The coverage on that was iffy, too. That's what she got for going with a lean insurance plan. Shrapnel, pieces of junk raining down on her vehicle, from an explosion wasn't in the standard coverage.

She wanted to scream. Release her frustration somehow. But before she got the chance, her cell rang. She didn't recognize the number.

"Cobie MacBride," she answered.

"Miss MacBride," a male voice said.

Her skin crawled. "Who is this?"

"My name is Gerry Wainwright. I'm the CEO of Deep Water Marine Salvage and captain of the *Voyager*. I received an interesting phone call this morning from Dr. Cooper."

"Oh?" Cobie's heart jumped.

"First, let me say I'm very sorry to hear about your father's death."

Cobie pursed her lips. She believed the body was her father's, but what if she was wrong?

"Thank you, Captain Wainwright. What can I do for you?"

"It's what I can do for you. I called to extend you an invitation to see the salvage project your father assisted me with."

Cobie itched to ask the captain what really happened. Wanted to hear him tell her that her father hadn't been fired from the project. But she sensed she'd get much more information in person. "Thank you, and I accept your invitation."

"Good. How soon can you be ready?"

"I'll be there as soon as you give me the exact location and I can make the travel arrangements." She had a friend with a boat, but she wouldn't mention bringing that friend. Didn't want to risk Captain Wainwright reconsidering the unusual and generous offer.

"I hope I don't have to tell you how important it is to keep this to yourself. The location of the shipwreck is not a secret, but we don't want to broadcast what we are doing here. Trade secrets and the like. Knowing we're hoping to extract gold bullion, its value, could cause…let's just say…problems for us."

Cobie suspected she knew exactly what kind of problems he meant.

Adam shifted in his seat when he saw Cobie exit her house. He'd meant to be gone at sunrise, but like an idiot, he'd nodded off, overcome by a long night of watching the house. He couldn't believe that it was already nine o'clock in the morning. Chief Winters assured him he would have police cruisers drive by, patrol the area often, but that wasn't enough for Adam. He'd seen a cruiser twice last night. That was all.

He didn't think it was enough for Chief Winters, either, but the man had more than Cobie to look after. Mountain Cove PD was still immersed in damage control after the fires and gang members who'd come to town and attempted to hurt or kill people close to Tracy Murray. And now Cobie was in danger.

He remained shaken from the bomb that had taken her business and almost taken both their lives. There wasn't any way Adam could sleep at home, much less travel abroad, knowing what she had been through and what was still to come. If only she would agree to stay at his grandmother's until this was over.

But there she was leaving her home, and she was sure to spot him. He knew she wouldn't be happy with his hovering. She craved normalcy in her life.

Fat chance. She wouldn't get normal until this was over.

He thought about backing up or driving off, but that might draw more attention to himself. When she opened the door of her rental car and then looked up, searching the area, her gaze landed on his truck. She slammed the door and crossed the street, marching up to him.

Oh, here it comes.

He stepped out of his truck to face the wrath.

She planted her hands on her hips. "Just what do you think you're doing?"

He could tell her that he'd just gotten here. But dishonesty never worked. It was the truth or nothing. "Watching your house, that's what. You gotta problem with that?"

"The only problem I have with it is that you didn't

tell me you were going to. I could have gotten some sleep if I'd known you were here. But no, I just laid there and stared at the ceiling. Freaked at every noise."

"Now you're making me feel bad. I didn't want you to be upset that I was watching. I guess I didn't think it through. So now you know that from now on, until this is over, I'm going to watch over you, Cobie MacBride."

It's what her brother would have wanted. He'd keep drilling that into his head until he believed it was the only reason he was here. That he wasn't here because Cobie had gotten under his skin years ago and never left. He couldn't let it be about that.

"Adam Warren, you're not superhuman. You can't stand guard every minute of every day." She dropped her angry stance. "But I'll take what I can get, and thank you."

Adam couldn't believe his ears. Then he saw it. Something had changed in her demeanor. "Something's happened?"

"Yes." And that smile he'd always loved graced her lips.

Adam's pulse jumped. Because of her smile. Because something had happened to make her smile. "What is it?"

"We're going to the shipwreck, Adam. Only you're probably too tired to go with me because you were up all night."

"Weren't you?"

"You've got me there. But I'm too excited to feel tired right now."

"Tell me."

"The details?" Cobie relayed that the salvage company owner had invited her after her contact with the state archaeologist.

"Are you sure this is a good idea?" Adam wasn't certain he liked how quickly it had all come together. "Smells fishy to me."

"Exactly. And I'm fishing, aren't I? I'm looking for answers."

Frowning, Adam scraped a hand through his hair. He needed a shower and a shave. What was new?

"What am I supposed to do, not go?" She quirked a brow. "It's safe, Adam. This invitation came through me contacting the state archaeologist."

"I'm not saying it's not safe." At least he didn't think that's what he was not saying. He grimaced. "I'm tired and I have a headache and—"

And now he was whining too much for his own ears.

"And you need some coffee."

"That I do, but…where were you going just now?"

"To find you. I couldn't get you on your cell."

Adam reached back into the cab of his truck and found his cell phone was dead. No wonder she couldn't reach him. Embarrassed, Adam grabbed his charger and shut the truck door. "Why don't you gather what you need and I'll wait for you inside. Then we'll get my stuff. In the meantime, it's my guess that you're going to need a boat."

"You guessed right."

"I think I can handle that end of things."

"I was hoping you'd say that." She smiled.

He grinned back, liking that she was finally learning to rely on him, lean on him, if only a little. "I'll make the arrangements, then, to take us to the shipwreck salvage site."

And he'd make sure Chief Winters, Ray and his brothers knew what they were doing and where they were going.

Just in case.

FOURTEEN

"I don't know if this is the right idea. The direct approach would have been much better." On Superior Island, Cobie waited next to Adam, hidden behind trees as he peered through binoculars at the *Voyager* anchored in the waters of Chambers Passage. She wondered if Deep Water Marine Salvage would have to give up their efforts in the coming winter months. Maybe the vessel was capable of weathering the rough waters.

Adam didn't respond, just kept looking.

She tugged on his jacket. "Did you hear me?"

"Yep. And we'll take the direct approach after I get a look at what we're walking into. The lay of the land—or rather the boat."

Since they'd been invited to the salvage vessel, Cobie wasn't comfortable with Adam's cloak-and-dagger methods. They'd taken the Warren family boat, and Adam had opted to anchor a couple of miles down on the opposite side of the island, away from the channel where the *Voyager* was anchored.

Then they'd had to hike through the woods. Adam had wanted to observe things from a distance and then make their approach.

"We've been invited. This is just…well…rude."

"Nothing wrong with being cautious, especially in light of the fact someone tried to kill you, and we found your father's body in that cave. Your father was fired from his job on the *Voyager*. That's why we're starting here."

"You don't have to make me feel like an idiot, repeating what I already know." She blew out a breath. "But you're right. Nothing's wrong with being cautious. Yet even though I think Dr. Burkov lied about my dad getting fired, that doesn't mean I suspect the salvage company had anything to do with his death or with the attempts on my life, okay?"

Adam dropped the binoculars and eyed her. "That remains to be seen."

"Give me those." She yanked the binoculars from him, peered through them and got a closer look. The binoculars didn't reveal much. She'd already seen the remotely operated underwater vehicle, the ROV. The *Voyager* was a good eighty feet or so, bigger than Cobie had imagined it would be. It looked like a research vessel she'd seen on the Discovery Channel. For some reason she'd pictured a much smaller boat, retrofitted for surveying or blowing, since Chambers Passage wasn't exactly ocean deep. She'd done a little research on the SS *Bateman* and the boat was 250 feet deep at the bottom of the passage.

"Looks like some serious salvage business down there." She handed the binoculars back to Adam. She thought back to what Yuri had said about the gold and wondered if they had discovered it yet. He'd never really said. Maybe he didn't know, considering everything seemed so secretive. One thing was certain; she wouldn't find the answers standing here and watching from the sidelines. The various police entities were too far removed to investigate and dig deep enough.

"You're not kidding."

"And I'm eager to meet them. We won't find the answers until we do." *And maybe not even then*.

The snap of a twig snatched her attention. Cobie turned around and faced off with the muzzle of a gun.

"Whoa!" Adam immediately threw his hands in the air and stepped in front of Cobie. "What do you think you're doing?"

"I could ask you the same." The man wielding the weapon looked like a bouncer who should be standing at the entrance to a bar rather than the woods on this remote island. Wearing a gray jacket over a black turtleneck, he was bald and his neck was as thick as his biceps.

"Minding my own business, that's what I'm

doing." Adam didn't want to agitate the guy, but neither did he want to admit to spying. And really, what law was there against being observant?

Using the gun, the man pointed at the binoculars. "Right, and I'm knitting socks. I heard you talking. So you're going to need to come with me."

"We're not going anywhere." Adam stood his ground and lowered his hands.

His own gun was hidden beneath his jacket. If he needed to, he could get to it, but he hoped it wouldn't come to that. Someone could get hurt or die, and he'd been party to too much death already.

"Look, this is all a misunderstanding," Cobie said.

"I don't think so." The man narrowed his eyes, directing his next words to Adam. "Now carefully pull that weapon out and toss it."

Grinding his molars, Adam did as he was told. "Can you at least tell us what you think is going on? Who you think we are? Because I'm telling you we're just out exploring the island. You have no reason to do this."

"That'll be up to the captain."

Adam shared a look with Cobie. "The captain?"

"Owner of Deep Water Marine Salvage and captain of the *Voyager*, the vessel you were spying on."

"This is all a big mistake," Cobie said. "We were invited by Captain Wainwright."

"Then you won't mind coming with me. You," he said to Adam. "You lead the way."

"I'm Cobie MacBride, and this is Adam Warren. The captain isn't going to be happy with how you're treating his guests."

"Guests that are spying. We've had enough trouble. If you're legit, then we'll find out soon enough."

"There's no need to brandish a weapon either way. There's no law against us looking through binoculars. We were simply looking to make sure that we had the right place."

Adam held his tongue. Cobie should stop talking, too. This man didn't seem like the kind of person who would be involved in salvaging a shipwreck. An image of Cobie's father flashed in his mind. Scientists, archaeologists and students came to mind for this type of project. Not trigger-happy thugs.

Regardless, they'd been caught, and Adam had made a mistake. She'd been right to insist they should take the direct approach. Not that this guy would seem any less menacing if they'd seen him while approaching the boat head-on. Either way, they were heading for the boat now, and they were in it for the long haul.

Adam led them through the woods as he was directed, down to the shore, where a small boat was beached. Their escort must have seen Adam's boat and come to investigate, sneaking up on them from behind.

"Can you put the gun away now?" Cobie asked. "We're going willingly because we were invited. We were on our way there. You don't need the gun."

He held his palms up, and the weapon, too, as though surrendering. "I was hired to do a job. Protect assets. You two were spying, and you can't deny it. But I'm not going to hurt you unless you give me a reason, so you can quit worrying. Now, do you want to meet the captain or not? If you don't, then this is your chance to walk away, but you'll need to leave the island."

"We want to meet the captain, but my boat is just on the northeast side of the island."

"I can't take you there in this. I'm almost out of fuel. And I'm not tromping across the island, either. How about we come back for your boat."

"So how about you give me my gun back?"

"All in good time."

With everything that had happened, Adam didn't trust anyone, but this man appeared to be what he said he was—security. And that brought to mind a question. Why did the *Voyager* need security? Had they indeed found the almost mythical gold that Cobie had told him about? He wanted to ask the man but didn't want to press him or cause them any more trouble.

At least everyone that counted knew that Cobie had come to visit the site and planned to stay a few days in order to see everything—the state archaeologist that had made contact with Wainwright on Cobie's behalf, Chief Winters and Ray. Adam wouldn't have come without getting the go-ahead from Ray. His friend had been reluctant, but Ray had admitted the authorities were no closer to solving the mystery of her attacker on the island and/ or any possible link to her father's death. *Voyager* seemed to be their best chance of getting some answers. It was clear something major was going on here. Why else would Bouncer believe he should hold them at gunpoint for simply observing?

Adam and Cobie climbed into the small boat and let the man take them to the *Voyager*, which was even more impressive up close. Once they reached it, Cobie climbed aboard, assisted by a man in tan coveralls and a blue helmet, and then Adam followed close behind, Bouncer on his heels. Adam stood near Cobie to protect her and watched Bouncer tuck his gun away quickly. Adam's, too.

He wanted his weapon back.

A couple of other guys, also wearing blue helmets and orange life jackets, joined the guy in the coveralls. They looked like mechanics or construction workers. Maybe they were exactly that and worked on the vessel itself. Beyond them, Adam spotted a couple of guys in diving gear who had stopped to look. A woman stood next to the ROV. All eyes were on Cobie and Adam.

Bouncer didn't bother to introduce them, but gestured toward the pilothouse, a couple of levels up from the deck. Cobie and Adam climbed the stairs, clanking as they stepped all the way up. Finally they entered the wheelhouse. Two men stood deep in a heated conversation. The one facing Cobie and Adam stopped when he saw them, triggering the man with his back to them to turn and face them.

He wore a navy blue windbreaker and a tan ball cap over silver hair. He studied them with his dark brown eyes and almost smiled. Then he frowned at Bouncer.

"Caught them spying from the island," Bouncer said, a hint of defensiveness in his voice.

Holding a steaming cup in one hand, the man ran his other hand over his clean-shaven face. "Spying, Jim?"

"They were watching the *Voyager* through binoculars."

"There's some mistake. Captain Wainwright, isn't it?" Adam said, assuming he was the captain. "You invited us. This is Cobie MacBride, and I'm her friend, Adam Warren."

"Well, why didn't you say so?" The captain thrust out his hand and gave Adam's a good hard shake. "Gerry Wainwright. Owner and CEO of Deep Water Marine Salvage and captain of the *Voyager*, at your service."

The gesture warmed Adam, made him believe

in the man's honesty. He appeared genuine to the core. Cobie offered her hand, too. Smiling, the man shook it, but not quite as hard.

"And this is Chad Tombs. He oversees all the operations—the dive crew, archaeologist, recording the data and all the technical stuff. Kind of my right-hand man, if you will."

Wainwright looked to be in his sixties and Chad not much younger. Adam figured it took years of experience all over the world to get to the place these guys had achieved. Cobie and Adam shook hands with Chad, as well. When introductions were over, the captain set his mug down and jabbed his hands in his pockets.

"We stopped at the island," Adam said. "Took a walk and scoped out where we were headed with the binoculars. Then Jim held us up at gunpoint and practically forced us here." Though to be fair, he'd given them a choice when they got to the boat.

Wainwright laughed, as though trying to make light of things. "Well, at least you're here. I apologize for Jim's overreaction and hope you'll forgive his indiscretion."

"I was just doing the job you hired me to do." Jim definitely sounded defensive.

Wainwright gave Jim a pensive look behind his smile and then turned his attention back to Cobie and Adam, appearing genuinely pleased that they were there. "It's been a long hard road to this point.

Took years to raise the money. A year more to get the permits. And then a competitor sued us, claiming they had the right to salvage the SS *Bateman*. We won in court, but it cost us more money than I care to think about. Since then, our competitor has been harassing us. We've had what looks like sabotage. A person can't be too careful. So maybe that'll help you understand Jim's knee-jerk reaction when he saw you with binoculars watching the *Voyager*. Not so easy to keep what we're doing here in the channels of these waters a secret, but we can try."

Cobie glanced at Adam. "I think we can let it go. We understand that he thought he was protecting your project. Don't we, Adam?"

Adam shrugged. It made sense, but he wasn't ready to let go of his wariness completely.

Wainwright's eyes grew serious, and he focused his attention on Cobie. "I was sorry to hear about your father. Tell me—how did he die?"

"We don't know yet. We're waiting to hear what the medical examiner says. I'm hoping to find answers to what happened. I thought starting with the last place he worked, well... It would be a start in finding closure for me personally, you see. If there's anything I regret it's that we'd been estranged for the last few years. I appreciate that you've allowed me this chance."

Adam cringed inside. They'd agreed they wouldn't reveal the true reason for their tour of the vessel—to find a link to what happened to her father, be it murder or otherwise. This visit was supposed to be about Cobie remembering her father. Finding closure. Despite the small doubt Chief Winters had planted regarding ID'ing the body, Adam believed Cobie's assertion that it was her father. And now what she'd told Wainwright might have been too close to the truth. He gauged Wainwright's reaction.

The man cocked his head back, measured Cobie. "It's been six months since your father worked here. We have a new archaeologist that took his place. I hope you find closure, but I'm afraid you won't find the answers to what happened to your father here. Likely just more questions."

Given that Wainwright came across completely transparent, warm and genuine, Adam found himself surprised to hear the man lying. He reminded himself to remain wary and distrusting. Regardless of what Wainwright said, there were answers here, all right. The only question Adam had was if they would be allowed to find them.

FIFTEEN

"All the same, we'll give you a tour, after you sign a nondisclosure, of course, and we'll even answer your questions, as best we can."

Cobie couldn't help but wonder if the man was going out of his way to make it look as though he wanted to help her so that she would move on in her search for answers. Or was the helpfulness because Dr. Cooper had pressured Captain Wainwright? She couldn't be sure. Beneath the captain's warm gaze, Cobie thought she saw understanding and compassion.

"I can't thank you enough for inviting us. For letting me see what my father had been working on."

"I understand what you might be feeling."

"You do?"

"I have a daughter in the Lower 48. My job was hard on the family and eventually led to divorce. I love my daughter, but the distance makes it hard to keep in touch. I'm a grandfather now, but I rarely get to see the kids."

His gaze drifted to something outside the windows. Was he thinking of the family he'd left behind while pursuing his career dreams? Yes, Cobie thought, this man did understand something of her situation. He probably understood her father, as well. They were two of a kind.

Cobie shared a look with Adam. Nerves. He was all nerves and, well, maybe some brawn. She was glad he'd come with her. She couldn't have done this alone, and she felt safe with him. As if no one could harm her. Not even Jim, the overreactive security detail.

The captain gave instructions to Jim and Chad. Then he smiled at Cobie and Adam. "Let me show you to your quarters so you can get settled and then you can meet the rest of the crew."

Adam scratched his head. "There's a problem. Our boat with our stuff is on the other side of the island. I tried to explain to Jim, but he claimed he was short on fuel and couldn't take us there."

"I apologize for the inconvenience. I'll show you to your quarters and have Jim take you to your boat to bring it closer and get your things."

"Adam and I can stay on his boat while we're here. There's no need for you to go to the trouble."

He lowered his chin. Looked at her. "I thought you might want to stay in your father's old cabin. But suit yourself."

"The cabin where my father stayed while he was

here?" Her breath caught. She glanced at Adam; the warning in his stern expression was clear. "I assumed my father took everything with him when he left, and that the new archaeologist was using the space now. Do you mean to say—"

"I'm not sure what he took, but what he left is still there."

"And you left it all there for six months?" She couldn't help how that sounded, but it seemed incredible.

"We should take this conversation elsewhere."

Cobie nodded and followed him, Adam behind her. They took the steps down inside the ship and Cobie had the distinct impression she was krill being swallowed down into the belly of a whale from which there could be no return. But she shook off the prickles of dread crawling over her and followed the captain. He'd been nothing but kind. She had no reason to doubt his sincerity. She guessed he was leading them to her father's quarters to speak in private. What had her father left? What did the captain know that he might share with them in private?

She couldn't help herself. She was nervous and excited about the possibilities and yet scared. Someone had tried to kill her. Someone was after something. But Captain Wainwright couldn't be the man who had attacked her. She sensed he was guiding her, trying to help her find answers. Maybe he wanted answers, too, about what had happened to the archaeologist helping him. Maybe her father and Captain Wainwright had even been friends.

Yes. Friends. She could easily see that now. Her father would have liked this man. Trusted him. She stumbled a little in the hallway, her hiking shoes catching. Adam caught her arm and assisted her, though she needed no help. But he took that opportunity to snatch her close and whisper, "Don't trust him, Cobie."

Ignoring him, she pulled away and smiled at the captain just as he turned to look at her. He stopped in front of a door and unlocked it. "We have five staterooms, and they can sleep up to three. And then we have crew quarters with bunks. Your father had a stateroom to himself."

When Cobie gave him a questioning look, he grinned. "We drew straws."

"Ah."

The captain gestured for her to enter first. He smiled, his eyes warm and friendly. He had a daughter. He understood Cobie's need to feel closer to her father. She stepped into the quarters and looked around.

Adam gestured for the captain to enter before him. She wanted to roll her eyes. He didn't trust the man, and she wouldn't, either, not with her life. With anything important. But still, there was no reason to be rude.

"I'm surprised that your crew didn't fight over this room after my father left."

Captain Wainwright's faced turned somber; then he turned to lock the door behind him. Was he afraid one of his crew would walk in on them? "It hasn't been easy. In a way I guess you could say I needed closure, too." He strode to a small desk with books and papers stacked on top and sat on the edge of it. "Please, sit."

Cobie took a chair next to the desk, and Adam remained standing. She couldn't wait to be alone in the room so she could go through her father's things. Glancing at Adam, she wondered if Wainwright had gotten his curiosity stirred, as well.

The captain tugged his cap off, and ran a swift hand through his silver hair. Cobie had half expected that he would be bald on top. A chill crawled up Cobie's spine.

The captain had the remnants of a bruise at his temple.

Adam spotted a bruise, right where Cobie claimed to have hit the man who'd gotten a choke hold on her. His gut tightened.

Wainwright had conveniently locked them in. What was he planning? Grabbing Cobie's hand, Adam intended to press her behind him and make excuses. They needed to leave.

"That's some bruise on your temple. What happened?" she asked.

Surprised, Adam squeezed her hand too hard, and she tugged it free.

"Accident with Sheba." He grinned. "I'll show it to you soon enough."

Adam cleared his throat. "Sheba?"

"The ROV. Remotely operated vehicle. You might have seen it on the deck. Only in our case, it's a remotely operated underwater vehicle. Was fixing the hydraulics and got slammed in the head. We call her Sheba. The Queen of Sheba brought valuables with her as gifts to Solomon. Gold and gems. And she brought questions with her." He grinned again, leaving Adam and Cobie to understand the comparison on their own.

Adam felt Cobie relax and then he relaxed slightly himself. His explanation of his injury was reasonable. The man was believable. If he had something to hide, he wouldn't have invited them. Would have kept his ball cap on to hide the bruise.

"You could have been killed," Cobie said.

"That's the truth of it."

"I take it you brought us here because you had something important to tell us." The guy might appear to be on their side and trustworthy, but Adam reminded himself he didn't know any more about Wainwright than he'd pulled up on an internet search. And that wasn't much. He wanted to get on with it.

"You have questions. I'd prefer you ask me rather than my crew. I don't want you getting them stirred up about what happened."

"Was my father fired?" Cobie asked.

"No." Wainwright slid off the desk and eased into the chair on the other side. "There was a disagreement, we'll just say. I told him to take a few days off to clear his head."

The man stared at them, as if waiting for them to add to the story. All of them waiting for the other to say something to fill in the missing pieces.

"And?" Adam asked, nudging Wainwright on.

"And he never came back. That was six months ago."

"I heard that he'd been fired," Cobie said. "But I didn't believe it."

Or she didn't want to believe it. Adam knew how it was when you wanted to think the best of a loved one. He and his siblings had looked up to their father, only to find out recently that he'd cheated on their mother two decades before, and the woman had been pregnant when she'd left Mountain Cove. Adam could have a half-sibling out there somewhere.

"You heard that? Not sure where you're getting your information. I guess that might have come from one of the crew who didn't know what was going on. With tempers flaring, arguments and such and then your father leaves and never comes back, people like to assume."

"You never said what the argument was about."

He narrowed his gaze. "No, I didn't."

There was a finality to his words, letting them know he had no plans to share the details of the argument. At least not yet.

"These things, the pictures on the walls, my father wouldn't have left them behind like this. Did you happen to call the police when he didn't return for them?"

"They came to us after someone close to him reported him missing." He quirked a brow at Cobie. "I answered their questions. Told them everything I knew."

Adam drew in a breath. The room grew too small and stuffy for him, and uneasiness settled like an anchor in his gut. He wasn't sure they should ask more questions just yet. Not until he got a better feel for things.

"Well, thank you for your answers. Cobie just wanted to—"

"Get closure," Wainwright interrupted. "I know why you're here. Maybe closure is part of it, I'll grant that, but you want to know what happened. I already told you that you won't find answers to those questions here."

Cobie shifted forward to the edge of her seat.

"You seem like a nice enough man. I figured you were friends with my father. I can tell he would have liked you. Won't you tell me what the argument was about?"

Women always thought they could appeal to a man's soft spot. Did Wainwright have a soft enough spot in his heart for Cobie because of his own daughter to give them answers now?

"Gold. The argument was over gold."

Adam had his answer about that. But then Wainwright tugged a gun from his pocket.

Adam prepared to step in front of Cobie. To wrestle the man. "What are you doing?"

"I'm giving you your weapon back." He handed it over to Adam, grip-first. "You might want to keep that on you at all times. I regret that Jim mishandled you, but we can't be too careful out here."

"Because of the gold?" Adam gripped his weapon, a sense of calm and control falling into place. It appeared that Wainwright really was a good man and had invited them here to help them. Maybe he wanted answers to what had happened to his archaeologist, as well.

"Yes."

"Did you find it yet?" Cobie asked. "I heard there have been many attempts to retrieve it. That it had become almost mythical."

"Miss MacBride—Cobie—you stay for a few days. Get a feel for the place and where your father worked. Get your closure, but the less you talk about the gold, the better, because there is no gold. Maybe I shouldn't have told you, but I've discovered I like you. Trust you."

He stood. "And you're right, I was friends with your father. But what's done is done, and I can't bring him back. I can't take back any words said aboard this vessel. So you see what you need to see, and then you leave. I don't need my crew getting distracted. Or to stir up what happened before. I invited you here partly to repay a favor to Dr. Cooper, the state archaeologist. And the other part of it is I know you need to see where your father worked."

But what were they salvaging if not gold? There had to be something of value, worth millions of dollars because this operation had already *cost* millions of dollars. They'd fought with another salvage firm for years. Cobie's father had argued with them over gold. Wainwright had said as much. Why argue over something that didn't exist? Adam wanted to ask, but he knew they wouldn't be getting any more answers out of Wainwright just now.

Adam stood, then grabbed her hand. "He's right, Cobie. Let's get a sense of your father's work here and then leave these men to do their job."

He had the keen sense that Wainwright was lying again, but about which part of the story, he couldn't be sure. Was it to protect Adam and Cobie, or to protect himself?

SIXTEEN

Cobie entered the quarters where her father had stayed and tossed her purse on the queen bed covered with a blue bedspread. Adam came in close behind her and dropped her bag next to the bed. He still lugged his own pack but would stow that in the quarters he'd share with other crew members.

"I don't think this is a good idea, Cobie." Adam stepped directly in front of her. Tried to burn a hole through her with his laser gaze.

Ignoring him, she moved by him and touched the wall where her father had pinned pictures. She slid her hand over the images. "He kept pictures of me...and Brad."

She turned to Adam then, sucked back unshed tears. "This is as close as I've been to him in years. It's pathetic, I know."

Dropping to the bed, she bounced a little and heard the mattress squeak. "And his things are in here. I can go through them. I can feel what he might have felt. I can see what he saw every morning and night. And maybe I can even get a sense about what happened to him. This is a gift from God."

"Cobie, what if someone here had a hand in his death? You could be in danger here. And I think Wainwright is playing you. Playing us. He's lying about something."

"Of course he's not telling us everything, but that doesn't mean he's lying. He doesn't want us to know what they're really after down there. And I don't care about that. I only care about my father."

"Your life. You care about your life, don't you?"

"You have your gun—he gave you the gun back. He wouldn't have done that if he didn't trust you. Chief Winters and Ray wouldn't have let us come if they thought we would be in danger. The police have already talked to Captain Wainwright and his crew. That said, I know we need to be careful. I know there has to be more to the story than he's telling us."

"There's definitely more. It's beyond strange that someone hadn't already claimed this room for themselves since most of them have to be sleeping two or more to a room. Maybe the crew has some sort of superstition about staying in the room of a dead guy, a murdered man. And in that case, they would have to have known what happened to him all along."

Cobie didn't like to hear that. "They're too modern, too technical to be superstitious like that. But I admit it's strange they left my father's things intact, including that trunk. Everything's left out like he intended to come back. I think… I think my father went to the cave before or after that argument. Then he went home to see Barbara, leaving his journal there. He must have returned to the cave for some reason…"

"But he never made it out of the cave." Adam stepped closer and ran his hands down her arms. "Someone didn't want you inside the cave because they knew you would find a body. Your father's body. We shouldn't stay here on the *Voyager* overnight."

Cobie wanted to be done with this conversation so she could open the trunk. Stick her hands in her father's things, his books, and feel close to him for a little while. But first she had to convince Adam they could stay. Convince herself a little, too. She turned to him, looked into eyes that conveyed tenderness and warmth. She could feel the heat coming off his body. The room was cold, and she wanted to melt into that heat, melt into him.

He frowned and didn't say anything else. Probably waiting for her to make her case. "I was on an island, Adam, when I was attacked. I was at work in my dental office when it blew up, and someone broke into my home. This is as safe as any place. And who knows? Maybe it's safer."

"If you ask me, we're being circled by killer

whales who just want to play with us before they eat us."

"Let's meet some of the crew, get to know them at dinner tonight, and then if you still feel uncomfortable, we'll stay on your boat. We can even take it down a ways and anchor there, just to be safe. Then in the morning we're back here. But he only gave us two days. I—"

"You really want to stay here. I get it." Adam reached forward and twisted a tendril of her hair in his finger.

The gesture was intimate. Stirred something in her. She closed her eyes and let the dizziness wash over her, thrill her. When she opened them again, it seemed Adam had inched even closer. Emotions poured out of his gaze. The room was small, like a tight space in a cave, and they'd been here before. Yes, she remembered it now. In a small, tight space staring at each other. She saw now what she hadn't seen then. Why hadn't she realized before— all those years ago when he looked at her—that he wanted her, too?

She saw it now in his eyes, that same look she'd seen before, and knew they'd both been dancing around her brother for different reasons. Brad had kept them apart then, and he was still keeping them apart now.

Adam was set to bunk with two of the crew in tight quarters that smelled like a locker room. No surprise there. He stowed his bag, hoping he and Cobie would leave tonight, hoping when they did he would leave with everything he'd come with. He tucked his weapon in his holster under his jacket and grabbed the SAT phone from the bag. He wanted to keep Ray updated with what was going on, and to do that line-to-site was necessary, which meant he needed to be outside. Fortunately, that would give him fresh air, too, but he doubted he would get any privacy to make his phone call. Wainwright might frown on his communications, too. He had no doubt the man was hiding things from them.

He made his way down the hallway and stopped at Cobie's quarters. He'd promised her he would be right back and together they would go up top and get the tour they'd come for. But when he knocked on the door, he got no answer.

Leaning his head against the cold door, he hoped to hear something inside. Maybe she'd fallen asleep. "Cobie, it's Adam."

Nothing at all. He blew out a breath and picked up his pace. Maybe he'd find her up top with Wainwright already starting the tour. What part of him saying he'd be right back had she misunderstood? He hated that they'd had to come here. Hated this whole thing. But considering the attempts on her life, this seemed like a logical next step. He agreed with her that it was better to be proactive than to sit back and wait for another attack when she had no idea what the people trying to harm her were after.

If anyone on this salvage crew had anything to do with her father's death, or the attacks on Cobie, they had already gone through her father's trunk and taken whatever was important or incriminating. She wouldn't find anything there. Wainwright wouldn't have invited them otherwise.

Adam climbed the steps and pushed the door open, hitting the light of a gray day, a bite in the wind foretelling colder and harsher weather to come in the next few weeks as autumn pushed into winter. That reminded him of his promise to his sister, Heidi, to be home for Christmas. Since he hadn't left Alaska yet, he wondered just where he'd be in the next few months. Where he'd have to travel home from for Christmas. This thing with Cobie would be wrapped up by then, no doubt, and he hoped and prayed it all ended well.

On deck he received a few looks. Rich and Penny stopped him and introduced themselves. They were two of four divers on the crew, though he learned that almost everyone on the crew had been a diver at some point in their treasure-hunting and salvage careers. Michelle operated the ROV via the joystick below deck, and Phil, the guy in the coveralls he'd seen earlier, was an all-around handyman. His three hard-hat buddies held things together, worked in the engine room, on the ROV, fixed mechanical problems.

Another man, lanky and midthirties, paused when he passed Adam on the deck. He had a Van-dyke beard, which gave him a sinister look. "Kevin Anderson." He grinned, taking the sinister out of his look. "I'm the archaeologist on this project. Glad to have you aboard."

Adam introduced himself and asked if Kevin had seen Cobie. "Yep. Met her, too. She's with Wain-wright looking at Sheba." He pushed by Adam and headed on his way.

Adam couldn't help but wonder if Kevin knew what had happened to the last archaeologist. But he didn't think about that long. He spotted Cobie stand-ing on the deck, looking out at the waters of the channel with Wainwright, who pointed at the umbil-ical cord attached to the ROV. He'd seen these kinds of operations on treasure-hunting reality shows, but never up close and personal. Still holding his SAT phone, he strode up to Cobie, hiding his displeasure that she'd taken off without him.

He squeezed her shoulder, forced a gentleness into his tone. "I knocked on your door. Thought you were going to wait."

"The captain knocked," she said. "I thought it was you. He invited me up to see the ROV."

Her face expressed an apology, and Adam couldn't hold it against her. Her eyes were bright, caught up in the thrill of this adventure. Had she forgotten the potential for danger? The threat to her life? Adam sure hoped not. But neither of them had expected that she would have the chance to stay in her father's old quarters, and that had thrown them off balance. Maybe too much.

Maybe Wainwright was counting on that.

Adam lifted the SAT. "I need to stay in touch with my business. I'm just going to make a call over there."

His business was to stay in touch with Ray, but Wainwright didn't need to know that. The man stiffened, but how could he deny Adam without casting suspicion on himself or the salvage crew?

"Don't you want to hear about the ROV?" he asked.

Adam would be more interested to hear how Wainwright could talk about the ROV without mentioning what they were really after.

"My call won't take long. I promise." And he'd keep Cobie in his sights.

Without waiting for approval he didn't need, Adam walked to the edge of the deck, keeping his eyes on everything, and frequently glanced back at Cobie and Wainwright. When he found a spot he thought would be reasonably private, he turned so he could watch Cobie and entered Ray's number.

Adam knew that his friend was busy working on a big drug bust that had bumped Cobie's father's investigation to the sidelines, but he trusted Ray to work on that at the same time as his other priorities. Ray would be there if they needed him. He left him a detailed voice mail, though there wasn't much to say other than they were on board and Wainwright was cooperating. He also mentioned that Cobie's father had left things behind.

Adam still wondered about the gold argument that had sent her father away. Why argue if there was no gold? When Cobie and Wainwright moved to the other side of the pilothouse, Adam could no longer see them. *Great.* He wanted to try the SAT again and talk to Ray in person if he could. Or wait for his friend to call him back. But instead he made his way around the deck to find Cobie surrounded by some of the crew he'd met, and some he hadn't— more technical types. Scientists or computer nerds, Adam guessed.

A smile on her face, she shot Adam a glance, nerves firing in her eyes. "And here's Adam now. I was just telling them we'd love to go with them to Joe's for dinner. It's their Friday night hangout."

"Maybe." Adam needed more information before he agreed. They had a few hours until then to decide.

"Almost everyone goes," Wainwright said. "Gets them off this boat for a spell so they can think clearly. We'll be shutting down this operation for the season in three weeks, so they'll have more time to think then."

That brought on laughter.

"What about you?" Adam asked. "Will you be there?"

"Me?" Wainwright shrugged. "I'm the part of the boat they want to get away from."

Guffaws erupted among the men; then they dispersed back to their chores. Adam noticed a man he hadn't met yet—someone who hadn't been circling Cobie—standing next to the wall, watching them. Watching her. When he saw Adam had noticed him, he slipped out of sight.

SEVENTEEN

They'd taken two small trawlers to Joe's, ten miles south on the east side of an island. As the wind whipped around her, Cobie was grateful for her jacket and tucked her hair in the hood. When she shivered, Adam stood behind her and wrapped both arms around her, cocooning her. She stiffened at first, not prepared to be so close to him, but then she accepted the additional warmth he offered as the boat sped through the channel waters. The sun began to dip behind the island mountains.

"Maybe we should go below deck until we get to Joe's." He spoke into her ear so she could hear over the wind.

"And miss all the fun?"

After a hard week's work, the crew reminded her of a bunch of crazed high school football players celebrating after their victory. Cobie wished she wasn't the only woman on the boat. Penny and Michelle were on the other boat, following not too far behind.

"We need to—" The wind caught his words.

"What?" she yelled.

"We need to leave tomorrow." He pressed his lips against her ear this time. She knew why—he didn't want the others to hear.

"Why? We have two days, just one additional night, Adam."

She felt him tense and could tell that something had him worried. Cobie knew what she wanted, but at the same time she trusted Adam. Trusted his instincts.

"Okay, tomorrow then. But tonight we stay on the *Voyager*."

He tightened his arms around her, snuggled his head close to hers, as if they were a couple, which they weren't. But in that moment it felt as though they were, and Cobie's conscience waged an ongoing battle with her traitorous thoughts. She wouldn't step away from the warmth he offered, the strength she got from being this close to Adam. If she went below deck to keep out of the wind and stay warm, that would mean that Adam would have no reason to wrap his arms around her and keep her warm.

Then the ride was over all the same, as the boat slowed and was steered into a busy dock. Lights and noise and music burst from Joe's a few hundred yards away. Adam helped secure the boat as everyone hopped off. Cobie wanted to wait for the two other women from the second boat. Penny smiled when she saw Cobie and grabbed her arm, dragging her forward into the restaurant. Michelle didn't have a warm personality, but she appeared to like Cobie, too. She glanced over her shoulder and saw Adam catching up.

Once they were settled at a long picnic-style table and everyone had ordered drinks, Cobie peered around the place as best she could. The owner kept it dark. She didn't like that it was much too noisy to have a meaningful conversation, her whole purpose behind coming. Still, she could listen to the others, pick up what she could and maybe ask questions about her father.

She reminded herself that someone had tried to kill her. Someone had come to her house. She'd seen that face in her window, and that person wasn't here at this table.

Adam sat directly across from her and talked to Chad Tombs, Captain Wainwright's right-hand man. The guy who was in charge of operations. Whatever that entailed. She trusted Adam to find out what he could, if the man knew anything.

Rich, one of the divers, sat to her right, but he was caught up talking to another guy she hadn't officially met. She decided to use the time to observe everyone.

Before her father had become distant, she'd been on a few field digs with him. Sometimes they included hired hands along with the college students and other experts—the PhDs and anthropologists alongside the archaeologists. But this marine salvage crew was nothing like what she'd experienced before. There was a different feel to this group of people, as if they were a different breed altogether with different wants and needs. This project wasn't about the history or the science, even though they had the scientists on board. It was about treasure hunting. It was about greed.

Her father hadn't been around much, but he'd made sure she understood the difference between archaeology and treasure hunting. He'd been part of this crew as their contract archaeologist, reporting their finds to the state.

As voices buzzed around her and the waitress took all their orders, Cobie thought about her father. Had he found something these treasure hunters hadn't wanted reported? Did that ever happen?

The drinks came—hot tea and coffee for her and Adam and beers around the table for a few of the others. They laughed, sang, enjoyed themselves, not acting anything like the savvy high-tech crew she'd met. And yet, despite the jovial atmosphere, they seemed wary.

Wary and trying to forget she and Adam were among them. Even Penny and Michelle had struck up their own conversation about the best shopping in Seattle—a conversation from which they excluded Cobie. Funny because neither of them looked like the shopping type, but to be fair, they were talking about the best place to buy hiking gear. Penny had long straight black hair, high cheekbones and looked like she might have native Alaskan blood in her. She was beautiful, natural and strong. Michelle had mousy dishwater blond hair and pale features, but she was also strong and had those intelligent eyes that could intimidate.

Looking around the busy restaurant, Cobie momentarily wished that she and Adam could grab a booth of their own and talk. She tried to remind herself that she didn't want more time alone with him. Being with him like this, seeing how much he cared and how far he was going to help her, she might actually have to forgive him. To let go of what happened. And Cobie didn't want to go that far, though as a Christian she knew she should. She wanted her anger and resentment. Those feelings were what had kept her from crumbling over her losses.

She prayed God would help her change—that was the one thing she was willing to do. But she couldn't think about her issues with Adam. Not now. They were here to do a job. Find out what happened to her father.

The food came, and Cobie ate and talked to Penny and Michelle. Rich finally struck up a conversation with her about her work as a dentist. But nobody talked about her father. She would think *someone* would have mentioned him. She waited, hoping she wouldn't have to introduce the topic. How would she bring it up or when? As the food was carted away and more drinks brought, she realized that some in the group might have had too much to drink. That could be an advantage to Cobie because maybe someone would talk too much.

She leaned in closer to Rich. He stared into his beer, looking dazed. Why anyone would want to feel that way was beyond her, but she would use it to her benefit if she could.

"So, what about this legendary gold that nobody has discovered?"

She'd meant to direct her question to him alone, but despite the noisy establishment, despite the many separate conversations, everyone at the table stopped talking. They looked at her, some with glassy eyes, making her uncomfortable. Had they all been waiting to hear that question? Had this merely been a ruse to get Cobie to talk, revealing what was really on her mind? And why had she asked about the gold? She wanted to know about her father.

She glanced at Adam, knowing they had all misunderstood her.

Someone snickered, and then the rest joined in laughter. Blew off her joke of a question. Rich grinned. "Do you know the story? This boat has already gone through many salvage attempts over the century. The bow was broken off, and that's where we believed the gold was. A lot of effort to get there and bring up the crates that should have held the bullion."

Cobie waited, knowing that Rich wasn't finished.

He glanced around the table, all eyes on him as though to silence him.

"Then, we bring it up—the gold, that is."

"Really? You found the gold?" Her heart jumped.

"No. It was nothing but boulders. We found rocks. If there *was* gold, someone had already taken it and replaced it with rocks. There's your legend." Rich got up and left a space on the bench. It was then that Cobie noticed a man at the end of the table on the other side, sitting with the crew of the *Voyager*. She hadn't met him yet. He wasn't laughing. Wasn't smiling. His gaze zeroed in on her and narrowed. Then he slid from the bench and disappeared into the thinning restaurant crowd.

His gaze directed her to follow. She was wary, but she wanted to find out why he hadn't joined the rest in laughing off the gold. There was no gold, she'd been told, repeatedly now.

Another man—she didn't think he was part of their crew—plopped onto the seat next to her. He got in her face, much too close, and she smelled his sour whiskey breath. He slipped his hands in and around her waist to pull her closer, a crooked-tooth grin on chapped lips. "Hey, baby, how about you and me—"

"What are you doing?" Cobie tried to free herself from his grasp.

* * *

"That's it." Adam yanked the man's hands off Cobie, somehow extricating her from the drunk's hold without shoving the man off the bench.

He hadn't come with them from the *Voyager* and had been watching their group from the bar of the restaurant. Apparently Rich getting up was the opportunity he'd been looking for. The man laughed as if it was a joke. Would he remember his behavior tomorrow? Not that it mattered. Cobie and Adam wouldn't be coming here again. He pulled Cobie to her feet, and they grabbed their jackets.

"Let's get some fresh air." He ushered her out the door into the night.

Breathing easier, he relaxed and took her hand. "Are you okay?"

"Yes. Thanks for your help, but I could have handled him. He was drunk, didn't know what he was doing."

Adam wouldn't say anything else. He didn't want to argue. He just wanted to leave. Get out of this situation completely. He led her to a dimly lit pier to look out on the water. Lights flashed across the channel from another island. It was a beautiful night, and the peacefulness of it washed away the experience inside the restaurant.

Next to him, Cobie blew out a breath and relaxed. In any other situation, she would never hold his hand, lean up against him like this. When this was all over, it was going to blow up in both their faces, leaving shrapnel in his heart.

"I think you're right, Adam." She released his hand. "We should leave in the morning."

He sighed in relief. "I'm glad. And don't worry—we can take your father's trunk, all his stuff. Better for you to look through it at home." Though home hadn't been the safest place, either. Where? Where could she be safe if she wouldn't agree to stay at his grandmother's?

Voices erupted near the door of the restaurant. Adam glanced back, saw the man who'd been hitting on Cobie searching for something or someone in the night. Adam inched closer to her and took her hand again as though she belonged to him. He hoped he wouldn't have to fight the man over Cobie. "Let's make them think we're together, for your safety."

"Okay." Her breaths came faster, as if it took an effort to pretend. To hold his hand. "I can do this. Compared to what we've already done today, this is nothing. I can't believe we made it this far, Adam. That we're actually here and doing this. Trying to find out what happened to my father and why his body was left in a cave. I keep thinking one of the crew must know *something*. They seem like good people. Here to do a job. They're treasure hunters, and it's hard to imagine any one of them would kill someone."

Right, he would agree but when it came to millions of dollars, all bets were off. "Okay, so if we believe them that they came to find the gold and came up empty-crated, then what about the argument your father had over the gold? Why would an argument about gold that doesn't exist send him away?"

"I think there's someone who wants to tell me something. He was at the table watching me. He seemed to be set apart from the others. And then he left."

Sensing someone approaching, Adam glanced back to watch for any threat. Seeing a couple of the guys, hands thrust in their pockets, taking a walk, he slipped his arm around her, pulling her in nice and tight. He liked the feel of her against him too much.

Cobie.

The woman of his dreams.

The girl he'd climbed into this nightmare with.

He didn't like the sound of this mystery guy. "Who are you talking about?" Was it the same guy who had slipped away on the *Voyager* when Adam had spotted him?

"One of the crew I hadn't met yet. At the table tonight. He sat at the far end. He was watching me, didn't laugh about the gold. But the way he watched me made me think he was trying to send me a message. He wants to talk to me—I could sense that much."

"As long as you add an 'us' to that, then I think it's a go. We'll get this guy alone and see what he can tell us before we leave tomorrow."

"I pictured my father sitting there at the table, eating with them, day in and day out. Talking to them. Getting caught up in the love for his work. His presence here was for a different purpose than theirs. But I got a sense of him. I think I understand better now than I did why he committed so much of himself to his work. His job always took him away from us when we were kids. It led him to leave us behind with a nanny to raise us. That's why I wanted a career that was safe and stable and secure so I could go to bed every night in my own house. I didn't want the kind of job that would make me travel or leave a family behind." Her laugh was a scoff. "A family I don't even have. A family I'll probably never have."

He squeezed her tighter, hating to hear the words. Why did she say them? Before he could ask her—not even sure he wanted to go there with her now—she spoke again.

"The police might have questioned the people on the *Voyager*, but they didn't have a body at the time. Given what little we've learned, his job here could be tied to his death."

He concurred, but he didn't think it was a good idea to talk so plainly about it out in the open.

Adam peered over his shoulder again to get the

lay of the land, make sure nobody was approaching them, hoping nobody had overheard her. Then he saw someone standing in the shadows, watching. The man disappeared into the darkness. Just like on board the salvage vessel. Was it the same person? Either he had something to share or he had something to hide. What Adam desperately needed to know—whatever his secret—was it something important enough to kill for?

EIGHTEEN

Standing on the boat headed back to the *Voyager*—
the second boat this time, following the first—
Cobie noticed the stars were brilliant. The clouds
had cleared out, giving them a break from the rain.
Were they more brilliant than usual? Or was it just
that she appreciated them more when Adam tugged
her closer in his embrace? She wasn't sure how or
why she'd ended up in his arms on the boat ride to
Joe's in the first place, but here she was again. She
hadn't refused the warmth then and wouldn't refuse it now.

As for her growing attachment to him, she'd ignore addressing that for the moment. She needed
Adam in this with her, and he'd assured her he
would be. And then when they came to the end of
it, then she'd say goodbye. Cobie squeezed her eyes
shut, trying to barricade her heart from the hurt.

But what would hurt worse? The pain that would
come from pushing him away? Or the pain that
would come from keeping him close?

Her jumbled thoughts made her uneasy when she was this near him. She shrugged out of his arms and glanced back. "I'm not so cold anymore."

Just as she wrapped her arms around herself, the boat slowed and the engine sputtered. Adam's eyes grew wide; then a frown settled in. "I'd better go check. See what's going on. You stay right here."

She nodded. "I'll be fine. I'll talk to Penny and Michelle."

Next to the railing, the women huddled close, and Cobie made her way to them. "What do you think's going on?" she asked.

"Sounds like engine trouble to me." Michelle rubbed her gloved hands together. "We're about seven miles out. The first boat'll miss us soon enough. They'll drop some people off, then come back to get us. In the meantime, I'm going below deck. You guys want to join me?"

"Not a chance. Too much noise and too many smelly men down there." Penny cracked a smile at Cobie.

"Suit yourself." Michelle disappeared down the steps.

"You've got a nice one there."

"Who me? I have a nice what?"

"Your man. I'd say he's a keeper."

"Um, we're not really together. Not like that." Sounded stupid considering Adam held her as though he cherished her. "He was only keeping me warm."

Cobie didn't want to think it was anything else, anything more.

"Right. Well, you could have fooled me. If you're not together, maybe I'll have a go at him. That is, unless you have a problem with that. At the very least, you're friends, so you might have a say."

"That's right. We're friends. My brother was Adam's best friend growing up. He's... Brad died several years ago."

"I'm sorry to hear that." Penny didn't say more, and Cobie didn't offer. "Well, what do you say?"

"Pardon?"

"What do you think about me making a pass at your friend?"

Cobie didn't know how to answer. She didn't want a relationship with Adam, did she? Not anymore, even though she'd longed to have that with him almost her entire life. But she didn't think she could stand by and watch the exotic Penny make a move on Adam, either.

Her long black hair spilling out of her hood, Penny laughed and winked. "I'm only teasing. I couldn't help myself. Even though you might believe you're only friends, I see the way he looks at you. Better not let that one get away. It's a good thing for you that I like you—otherwise, I really would try to steal him away. In my field, it's not easy to get out and meet nice men."

"Oh." Cobie couldn't respond without showing her irritation. Maybe she should change the subject. "What about my father? He was nice to you, right? Tell me what you know about him."

Penny stared up at the stars, as though she had to think about the best way to answer Cobie's question.

Finally she dropped her gaze to Cobie. "You have his eyes." She shivered and rubbed her arms beneath her jacket. "He worked hard, was a good man. Was serious. Yeah, that's it… He was serious about his work. Didn't laugh or joke around. Kind of like you."

Penny couldn't know that his seriousness was because he'd lost so much, carried too much sorrow in his heart. Was that happening to Cobie? She'd promised herself she'd never forget what happened to Brad. Never forget Adam's part in it. But she was beginning to see that if she didn't let go, she'd end up cold and bitter. Unable to smile or laugh or enjoy life.

Unable to have a deep, meaningful relationship.

Penny squinted her eyes and looked beyond Cobie. She suddenly stiffened. "I'm going down below. It's too cold out here, after all. See you later."

When Cobie glanced over her shoulder, she saw him watching from the bow—the same man who had watched her before. Was he the reason Penny had suddenly opted to go below deck?

Cobie should follow Penny. That would be safer than standing out here alone. But she worried about Adam. Then she saw him and two other men with a hatch propped up, tinkering with the motor probably. She decided now was a good time to talk to the man who hadn't laughed about the gold. She could at least get his name.

Adam stood tall and searched the deck, his eyes landing on Cobie. She gave him a little wave to let him know she was okay, then sauntered over to the man.

He stood at the rail, looking into the dense black waters of the channel. Lights flickered in the distance on an island. Stars still twinkled in the sky—an unusual cloudless night.

"Mind if I join you?"

"It's a free world."

"I've met almost everyone on the crew, but somehow missed you. What's your name?"

"Mike Johns." Mike looked to be late forties, maybe fifty. He had that leathery look of someone who worked out in the sun a lot and only a little gray at his temples beneath his Huskies ball cap.

"What do you do on the *Voyager*?"

"I'm the guy they call when they need to use the magnetometer or side-scan sonars to locate the wrecks. There's a good three thousand shipwrecks along the Alaska coast, if you count all forty-four thousand miles of it. I also know how to use the survey software. Mostly I've been working as the data recorder. I worked with your father before he left."

Cobie's stomach rolled over. Finally she was getting somewhere, and she didn't want to scare him off. Of all the crew she'd met so far, this guy was by far the jumpiest. "Back at the restaurant tonight, you were the only one who didn't laugh about the gold. You were watching me. Why?"

"Like I said, it's a free world. Nothing wrong with a man looking at a pretty woman."

Maybe she'd misunderstood his reaction and the look in his eyes, but she didn't think so. "What can you tell me about my father? The captain mentioned that they argued over gold and then my father left and never came back. Why argue over gold when there is none, as the crew seems to believe? And if anyone would know whether or not there's gold, it would be the crew."

The man slowly pulled his gaze—icy and cold like the waters below—from the black depths and turned it on Cobie. "You have no business asking those kinds of questions. No business at all. But since you have, you need to watch your back. Rich told you we found boulders instead of gold. You think we're salvaging rocks down there?"

"I… I don't know, that's why I'm asking you."

"I thought you came here to see where your father worked before he died. Now you're a treasure hunter? Which is it?"

"My father. I want to know about my father. I don't care about the gold."

"Look, the best thing you can do is leave as soon as possible."

"I want to know why my father left and why he's dead. I'm looking for answers."

"Sounds to me like you have your answers. Your father asked too many questions, too. He argued over gold, and now he's dead."

Adam wiped off his oily hands with the rag offered, relieved they wouldn't have to stay out here much longer, surrounded by darkness. He just wished they were going somewhere other than back to the *Voyager*. Though he was exhausted, he wasn't looking forward to bunking with two other men on the crew. He would prefer his own bed on his own boat, but he understood Cobie's need to stay in her father's old quarters at least one night. And in the morning, they could more effectively gather his things and take them back to Adam's boat.

He spotted her—she'd moved to the bow. One more glance at the motor and he would close the hatch. Chad had left him alone and gone below deck for something. Adam dropped his flashlight, and got on his knees to search. Someone came up the steps from below. At first he thought it was Chad. But then Adam heard whispers.

"The only reason Wainwright invited them was to find out what her father had told her."

"Yeah, well, doesn't sound like she knows anything."

"She's fishing is all."

"Fishing isn't good. Means she suspects something."

"What do you think is going to happen?"

Adam's heart hammered against his rib cage. Who were these people anyway? What was really going on here? Adam didn't want to pop up and have them realize their faux pas, but what else could he do? He couldn't just remain on his knees hidden by the open hatch. They would notice him at any moment.

He jumped up. "Found it!" he exclaimed, making as much noise as he could so they wouldn't think he'd overheard their whispers. "Now she's purring like a kitten. Just needed a few more adjustments."

He didn't wait to see if they bought his act. He went in search of Cobie. They had to get away tonight.

Back at the *Voyager*, no one lingered around. Everyone stumbled into their quarters. Adam needed to get Cobie alone to tell her what he'd heard and about the man he'd seen watching them. The light was on in Wainwright's quarters near the pilothouse. Adam followed Cobie toward the light. Before he could stop her, she knocked softly on the door.

"Who is it?" Wainwright sounded irritated.

Adam held Cobie back. "Maybe he's readying for bed, and this isn't a good time," he whispered.

Her big eyes blinked at him. "We need to tell him our plans."

"Come in," the man behind the door called.

Adam shot her a warning glance. Unsure what they'd see on the other side of the door, especially knowing what he'd heard on the trawler, he needed to make sure it was safe. Thankfully, Cobie backed away. Cautiously he opened the door and looked inside.

Wainwright sat at a desk reading, his glasses halfway down his nose. Relief whooshed through Adam, and he hoped not visibly so.

The man glanced up and over his glasses. "I hope you enjoyed your evening."

Cobie and Adam came all the way into the comparatively spacious quarters.

"Yes, thanks." Cobie offered a soft laugh. "I enjoyed observing your crew. It was interesting, I'll say that."

He grinned, just barely.

"I wanted to let you know that Adam and I plan to leave first thing in the morning."

That got a reaction, and not just from Wainwright. Adam kicked himself on the inside. Adam needed to tell her what he'd learned. He'd been lost in his own jumbled thoughts trying to figure out how to keep her safe and how to talk her into leaving sooner. As in right away.

Flipping the book closed, Wainwright stood. He walked around the desk. "I'm surprised. I didn't figure you'd seen enough yet. Are you sure?"

"Yes, I'm sure. I appreciate all you've done, appreciate that you invited me. And thanks for letting me stay in my father's quarters. The things he left behind, getting those back… That's more than I could have asked for. I didn't realize you held on to his things. So after we load them—"

"Wait." He stiffened, stood taller. "I never said you could take his belongings."

"What do you mean? They belonged to my father, and now they belong to me."

As Cobie spoke, Wainwright shook his head. "They belong to Deep Water Marine Salvage. They're company property."

"Well, that doesn't even make sense. They can't be company property. He brought them here—they weren't issued to him. And besides, his clothes, his pictures, why would you want to keep them?"

Wainwright's face turned beet red. This was definitely a different side to him. "Your father took secrets with him when he left."

"I'm sorry, but I don't know what that has to do

with me. I didn't speak to him before he left. We hadn't spoken in months. I don't see what his things have to do with any of that. I could get a lawyer—"

"You *could* get a lawyer, but you'd be wasting your time and money—and for what?"

Exactly. What did Wainwright want with Cobie's father's things? Gone was the warm and friendly father-figure persona telling them things like, "See what you need to see. Get closure." In his place was a menacing man, intimidating and unyielding.

Adam gently squeezed Cobie's shoulder, wanting to reassure her, wanting to persuade her to give it up, because he could see that Wainwright wouldn't back down.

"The way I see it," he said, "you have two days and two nights to learn what you can about your father's stay here, and to go through his things while you're in his quarters. And please don't try to steal them, cart them off inside your luggage. We have a way of making sure people don't abscond with treasures when they leave, so we'll be sure to find anything you've taken."

"That's ridiculous!"

"However ridiculous it might seem to you, it's all detailed in the nondisclosure you signed."

"Just tell me why you want them! Why would you want to keep my father's things?"

"For the same reason as you. I'm hoping to find

something there, something I missed that will give me answers to my own questions."

"What questions could you have?" Adam stepped closer. "What aren't you telling us?"

Wainwright deflated, blew out a breath and then sat on the edge of his desk. "I'm trying to protect the both of you. But you're not making it very easy." To Cobie, he said, "Your father has something, or I should say *had* something, that someone else wanted—still wants, desperately needs. As long as his things remain here, that someone can't get to them. Would have to go through my crew to get to them. If you take his things with you, then you'll become a target."

Adam had had enough of this. "She is already a target. Someone tried to kill her and we're trying to find out why so we can stop this once and for all!"

Wainwright frowned, some of the man they'd met earlier in the day returning. "I'm sorry to hear that."

"Please," Cobie said. "Tell me what this is about. Then maybe I can help. You said my father argued over gold and then left, but the crew says there is no gold. If not gold, then what are you salvaging? Now you say my father knew something, a secret. What is it? What's so important that it was worth his life?"

Wainwright poured amber liquid into a shot glass, swirled it, then downed it. The guy appeared to grow more haggard by the minute. This dark secret, whatever it was, seemed to be devouring him before their eyes. "You're his daughter. I'm hoping you can find something that I missed, something only a daughter would know. You have a go at it and see what you can figure out. Until then I'm not letting go of the items in his room."

The journal.

Whatever he was looking for, her father had to have written it down in the journal. But Cobie said pages were ripped out.

"And then what?" Adam asked. "What if Cobie finds the clue that you need. What happens to us?"

Wainwright looked pained. "You don't need to be afraid of me. I'm just trying to run a business. One of my crew, a friend—your father—died. Was killed, I believe. Your father was here, working for me, for some other reasons besides looking for gold. If you find anything at all in his quarters, anything remotely promising, tell me what it is. Then we'll both have the answers we want. You can go back to your life, and I'll go back to mine."

Once again, Wainwright was lying. Had been lying all along. At first, he'd claimed he didn't know what had happened to Cobie's father. *Now* he said he believed he was killed. Adam listened as Cobie agreed to help with Wainwright's search for answers. As soon as Adam had her alone in the hallway, he was all over her. "We're leaving tonight. Get your things."

"Are you nuts?" she hissed. "Tonight is all I have to go through my father's stuff, and you're going to help me. If there's something to find, then we'll find it."

"Wainwright's lying, Cobie. From the beginning, he's been lying to us. Tonight I overheard someone say the only reason he let us on board was to find out what we knew, if anything. What secrets your father had told you."

"And that's pretty much what he said in his office. My father died with a secret, and Wainwright, along with someone else, needs to know. It sounded like he didn't want me involved, but now that I am, we can work together. I can help him find out that secret."

"There *is* no secret. Not from him. Wainwright knows what he's looking for. A man like him doesn't run a successful salvage business by being unaware of what it is he is salvaging. That's how he garners the investors. So I repeat—he is lying. He knows. That said, what if what Wainwright is looking for was in the pages torn out of your father's journal?"

Adam wanted to kick himself repeatedly. He should have taken the time to find out more about this shipwreck online, to find out what it had been carrying besides gold.

"In that case, we won't find the answers. We'll never know."

In that case, we'll never know until we face off with the person who is trying to kill you.

NINETEEN

Her father's quarters smelled old and unlived-in. With Adam in the room with her, the space grew stuffy if not stifling. "Please, let's search through his things tonight, and then we're gone. I promise. If we find it, we don't even have to wait until morning."

Cobie scraped clutter—magazines and books and a calendar—off the trunk. She could look through them later, but right now she wanted to get into this trunk. She'd been itching to do that ever since she'd seen it. No doubt Wainwright had already searched the contents, so she wasn't sure what she could hope to find or what he thought she would find that he hadn't. She fiddled with the lock. Who had locked it? Wainwright?

Cobie straightened and looked at Adam.

He pushed a hand through his hair, clearly distraught. "If we find anything, we can't take it with us no matter what time of day or night, Cobie."

"We don't have to take it with us—we'll know. That's all I want, just to know."

"That knowledge could get you killed."

Cobie had to remember that Adam was in this with her. It could get them *both* killed.

"Why did we come here if not for answers? We are not obligated to tell Wainwright anything. But, Adam, if we leave without those answers, then we haven't accomplished anything, and we'll still be in danger. Someone is still out there trying to kill me. Now come on—let's hurry. Help me get this lock off."

"It's new. Wainwright must have the key."

"Why didn't he give it to us?"

"Who knows? But no amount of hitting it is going to break it free." Adam tugged his weapon out of his pocket.

"Wait, what are you doing? You're going to wake the entire crew if you shoot that off."

A soft knock sounded at the door.

"Who is it?" Adam and Cobie asked at the same time.

"Me."

The captain. Cobie glanced at Adam. Did he remember the key? Before she could reach for the door, Adam opened it.

The captain glanced up and down the hall. "Can I come in?" he asked quietly.

Adam stepped out of his way and motioned him

inside. Eyeing the trunk, the captain half smiled until his gaze fell on Adam's gun.

"I was going to shoot the lock off."

"Figured." With a sheepish grin, he tugged something from his pocket, then held it up. "Glad I remembered this before you woke the dead with your gun."

"Thanks." Cobie snatched it and wished him away, but he just stood there, looking at them. "I thought you'd already been through his things," she prompted.

"I have. Just stopped by to give you the key and wish you better luck than I had." He nodded and left.

Adam blew out a breath. "The guy rubs me the wrong way. I liked him to begin with, but I don't like the secrets. I don't like the lies."

Cobie dropped to her knees and opened the lock. Now...now she could open this trunk. She gazed at Adam, who sat in a chair. "If there's nothing in here that's going to help us, then why are my hands shaking? I don't want to get my hopes up."

"Then don't," Adam said. "Just open it already."

She lifted the lid. Pretty much what she expected to see—everything rifled through. Shirts, pants, jackets. She tossed the clothing out and found more books. Always books. Her father carried a library with him. "Maybe there's something in one of his books. He always took some with him wherever he went. I used to think he loved his books more than me."

"So maybe you're right and there's a clue for us in the books. Wainwright wouldn't have known what to look for, didn't have the patience for it. This is why he invited you. You're the only one who can find the answers now."

"If that's the case, then why did someone try to kill me?"

"That's why. You're the only one to unlock the answers to your father's death."

"So someone wants these secrets to stay secret. Someone else wants to uncover them." Cobie sighed. "Let's get started, then. You look through that stack of magazines and papers, and I'll look through books, give them a cursory glance, and then we'll trade. Let me know if you see anything."

"I'll look, but I have no idea what I'm looking for."

"That makes two of us. You've been around my family long enough, Adam. You would know enough to recognize something, at least more than Wainwright."

"I just wish we had some coffee."

"So go make some."

"Are you kidding? I'm not leaving you alone for one second. We stick together until this is over." Adam placed his weapon on the small table on top of a book.

Cobie made herself as comfortable as she could, which wasn't very, and started flipping through the first book. After a couple of hours, she wished they had made the coffee. She noticed that Adam struggled to keep his eyes open. What could be more boring than schlepping through old books when you didn't even know what you were looking for?

"Hey," Adam's voice jarred her.

Had she been asleep?

"Why don't we get a few hours of sleep, then start back. We don't have to leave until we get our answers, or until we've looked through everything."

"Yeah, I don't know what good I'm doing if I'm sleeping through half of it. But what about you?"

"I'll lean against the wall and catch a short nap, too. I'm not going anywhere—I've already told you that. I have a weapon to protect us in case anyone tries to get in." Adam reached over and checked the lock, then caught the extra pillow Cobie tossed him.

She plopped on the mattress to catch a couple of hours of shut-eye, and then they would get busy again. Almost instantly she was asleep. When she woke up—jolted awake by a noise that sent her heart jumping up her throat—the room was completely black.

Then something soft—a pillow?—pressed against her face, and Cobie fought to breathe.

Adam shook off the daze. Someone had meant to knock him unconscious with a blow to his head. *Cobie!*

He had to get to Cobie. Adam felt along the wall until he found the light switch. Then in one swift movement, he pushed to his feet, grabbed his gun and flipped on the light.

What he saw terrified him.

Someone hunched over Cobie, holding a pillow to her face as she struggled. Adam jumped the man and smashed his gun into the man's skull. The attacker released the pillow and stumbled backward, slamming Adam into the wall and knocking the gun from his hand.

Cobie screamed Adam's name. The ruckus was sure to wake up the others, and help would come. The man wore a mask. Adam wanted to pull it off. He tugged at it, fought with their assailant. Cobie approached from behind.

"Get away, Cobie—get away."

Cobie tried to reach the gun, but the brawny man pushed her away. And then he brandished a knife.

He thrust it at Adam.

Adam dodged the best he could, pushed back against the knife, but the man was admittedly stronger. The knife inched forward until the sharp edge of the blade was mere inches away.

Okay, Cobie, now would be a good time to help...

But where was she? Had the man hurt her when he'd knocked her away? That thought gave Adam the surge he needed, and he'd almost pushed the knife away when their attacker fell against him, knocked into him by a chair slamming into his back.

Cobie. She'd come to Adam's rescue.

But the knife…

The knife… Pain erupted in Adam's side.

The masked man climbed off Adam, then turned to stare at Cobie. He was going to kill her, and Adam's wound paralyzed him, momentarily shocked him. He tried to push up, started getting to his feet, blood oozing from the wound. The sounds of others approaching the cabin drew the man's attention to the door. He forgot about Cobie and ran out.

She started after him.

Adam caught her ankle and held. "Don't, Cobie! Don't go after him."

"But I have to get the mask off."

"He'll kill you. He wanted to kill you—don't you see?"

Cobie dropped to her knees. Her eyes widened as she realized he was badly injured. "Oh, Adam! Adam, stay with me… Help!" she screamed. "Help! Someone help us!"

The door burst open. Wainwright and others poured into the stateroom. His face paled. "Quick," he ordered the other men. "Get him to the lab. The medical supplies are there," he explained.

Adam wasn't sure he wanted any of them helping. Any one of the men here could have been the one who'd tried to kill Cobie, who had stabbed

Adam. But then, Wainwright was the only man who matched the height and build of the man he'd just fought with. Had he run out the door and pulled off his mask? Adam tried to get a good look at him as they wrapped his wound to staunch the flow, then assisted him to the lab. His clothes… What had the man been wearing?

He glanced back at Cobie and tried to keep from losing consciousness. The injury was a shock to his system; that was all. He wasn't going to die. He couldn't die; he had to keep Cobie safe. They had to solve this together.

And if he died, who else was there to help her?

"Cobie, stay with me." He wasn't supposed to leave her. He was supposed to watch over her. "Where are you? Stick with me."

Then someone touched his hand. "I'm here, Adam. I'm here."

The men laid him on a table. Men from the crew who had been keeping a secret, had been lying to them. Adam was at their mercy now. He glanced down at the wound. "It doesn't look that bad, not really."

"Shouldn't he go to a hospital?" Cobie asked.

"Probably," one of the men answered. "But it's more of a flesh wound, so he's in no real danger."

Hearing that, Adam breathed easier, and a new determination to get out of here surged, energizing him.

"Here's some pain meds, should take the edge off."

"No, I can't take those." They'd keep him from thinking straight. He and Cobie had to leave. Had to escape. "Just wrap me up. Stitch me up, whatever you need to do."

"Are you sure?" Rich looked down at him.

Rich was going to sew him up? Adam squeezed his eyes shut. Nothing he could do about it. "Do I have a choice?"

"No. We need to stop the bleeding."

He stole a few breaths, calmed his nerves. Put his trust in God, where it should have been already. He hadn't been thinking about God, much less trusting Him lately, he realized. Nothing like a close call with death to bring things back into perspective.

And with God's help, Adam could do this. He could get past the pain now that he knew the knife hadn't hit anything important.

Rich stitched him up, wrapped his wound and left him alone with Cobie. She took Adam's hand. He slowly sat forward, dizziness swimming in his vision. "We have to get out of here. Call the police."

"Yes. We do. But are you okay to go? We have to get our things and then—"

"Yes. No. Forget about our things. We're getting on my boat and leaving. We'll make the call then."

"Okay, but my purse, my wallet, your keys."

"Right, okay." He wasn't thinking clearly. "I'll be okay. Just need a few minutes to get it together."

"You need some water." Cobie opened a small fridge and pulled out a couple of bottled waters. "Here—this should help."

He sure hoped so. He took a few swigs. Slid off the table. He would think that others would be here asking questions. Maybe they already had, and Cobie had answered them. She walked next to him, keeping him steady. He didn't want to be weak. They couldn't afford for him to be weak until they were somewhere safe.

"I'm sorry I let you down," he said as they made the hallway.

"What? Adam, you saved my life."

The image of the man covering her face with a pillow knocked into him again, and he leaned against the wall.

"Adam, I'm worried about you." Her voice was shaky.

"It was a flesh wound. I got hit in the head, remember? That's some of it." He tried to shake it off. Squeezed his eyes to wipe away the blurriness in his vision.

They made it back to her father's old quarters. "This is a crime scene, Cobie, on many different levels. But we're not staying to wait for the authorities."

He lowered himself into the chair, wondering

where Wainwright was at the moment. Instructing his crew on what to say to the police? Or planning how to kill Cobie and Adam?

"We didn't get through the books, Adam, We didn't finish." Disappointment surged in her voice.

He hated hearing it. An image flashed in his mind. "Maybe we did find what we need, after all. While I was on the floor, fighting the masked man, I saw something. Wedged between the bed and storage compartment at an angle. It's not easy to see. I could only see it from the floor."

She gasped and dropped to her knees to look. "I… I don't see anything."

Adam took another swig of water. He'd get on his knees and show her, but he figured that would break open the stitches and the blood would start flowing again. "It's there. Come over here. Lay down right where I was."

At least someone had wiped up the blood while he was in the lab. If the police ever made it to this room, maybe they could grab prints. They wouldn't be happy that Cobie and Adam were back in there messing with things.

Cobie did as he asked, lying flat, her face against the floor. "Yes, I see something. It's at a weird angle and easily missed."

Cobie gripped and pulled it out. "I got it!"

She sat on the floor and leaned against the bed. "A book. Of course it's a book."

"The Romanovs?" Adam quirked a brow.

She glanced at him. "You don't suppose…"

She flipped through the book, and Adam watched her eyes, her beautiful eyes, skimming over the pages, her finger spiraling down each page as she searched. He suspected she already knew something.

"Didn't I tell you Wainwright knows very well what he's looking for in that shipwreck? Maybe there's gold, maybe there isn't, but that's not what someone is after."

Suddenly, Cobie stopped on a page. Her gaze shot up, zinged to Adam's. "There's an old newspaper clipping here about one of the lost Fabergé eggs. The Dancing Stallion," she whispered. "And I think I know who wants it."

TWENTY

A deep scowl carved the captain's features. Cobie didn't know if that was because of the attempt on their lives on his vessel or because Adam intended to whisk Cobie away and the captain wasn't ready to let them go. A terrifying thought.

The man hadn't believed her when she'd told him they hadn't found anything in their search of her father's room. It wasn't as though they'd had much time, and if Adam hadn't hit the floor the way he had, then they wouldn't have found the book.

That solitary book wedged between the bed and storage unit never to be seen again unless the room had been stripped clean. Or someone had lain on the floor in just the right position. They'd left it behind. Stuck it back in the same place they'd found it. She wasn't sure Adam was convinced they were onto something, but Cobie believed she'd found a piece of the puzzle. Believed she knew what someone was after now. And if she was right, she also knew who.

She and Adam could talk about it when they were safe and sound and away from here.

After a search, they carried their bags onto Adam's boat. The captain helped them shuffle from one vessel to the other, his crew watching them go from the deck of the *Voyager*. They appeared visibly shaken by the attempt on Cobie's and Adam's lives. No one claimed to have seen a stranger coming or going on the vessel. *That* Cobie didn't believe. Someone knew something. Or it was one of them. Someone who had a key to get past the lock on their door.

The killer was one of them.

"We've called the authorities. Shouldn't you wait to speak to them?" The captain made another attempt to persuade them to stay.

"No. We're not safe here." Adam tossed his bag, then grabbed Cobie's. "Tell them what you like. We'll answer their questions another time and place."

"Whoever tried to harm you is long gone."

"You said that no one could get inside. No one could get past your crew." Adam kept his voice low. "Have you ever stopped to consider it might be one of them?"

Cobie hoped the men and women on the deck couldn't hear him.

"No, I never have."

And with those words, Cobie believed Captain

Wainwright had known all along who had tried to kill her. But none of it made sense. If someone was looking for a Fabergé egg and believed she could help find it, then why try to kill her before she could share her information? Her head ached with trying to figure things out.

"We'll be in touch." Cobie tossed out a wave but couldn't manage a smile. The wind gusted around them, bringing a cold drizzle. Adam tugged his hood over his head, as did Cobie.

He started the boat and eased away from the *Voyager*, then turned his attention to her. "We'll be in touch?"

He lifted a brow; his pensive gaze peeked from beneath the hood at her.

"I couldn't think of anything else to say, and really, this probably won't be the last time we talk to him. We have to figure the egg out, Adam, and maybe we should have talked to him about that. He knows much more than he's saying."

"You think?" Adam's sarcasm rolled over her. "What we have to figure out is who wants to kill you. That's it. I don't care why at this point, though I know finding out the why will lead us to the who." Adam increased speed. "But odds are that the guy who came into the room and tried to smother you, who stabbed me, is the same man who tried to strangle you to death on the island. You say you know who wants the egg, if that's what we're talking about here. Who is it? Who is trying to kill you, Cobie? What does it have to do with the book we found?"

"I'm not sure anymore." And that was the truth. She needed to think on it before she threw what could be an innocent man's name out there. None of it made sense. "The man in the cabin had a similar build as Captain Wainwright, and the captain has that bruise on his temple, but I can't be sure. Can't be positive it was him. There were differences, too. It's hard to stay focused on the details, to remember, when you're fighting for your life."

Both attempts had been to cut off her oxygen. Who could it be? No matter what the captain was hiding, Cobie couldn't see him as a killer. She just couldn't. Maybe it wasn't in her nature to think the worst of someone who had warm eyes. A slow burn began at the back of her throat. Had her father trusted the wrong man? Someone who'd killed him?

And what if Adam had died all because of this treasure someone wanted? Cobie wasn't sure she could live with herself if that had happened. Nor was she sure she could keep her resentment and continue holding Adam responsible for Brad's death. The thought of losing him… Well, that nearly undid her. She wanted to reach for him, hold on to him like they'd done last night out of sheer necessity.

Cobie jammed her hands in her pockets instead. "How's your side?"

"It's better. I'll be okay. Grab me the SAT phone

out of my bag, will you? I need to call Ray and up-date him to the latest developments and that we're headed back to Mountain Cove."

Shivering, Cobie wiped the mist out of her eyes. She had the sense that danger was circling her, clos-ing in on her, and she didn't know if she would es-cape alive.

"Okay, I'm going to take the bags below deck, too."

"Thanks."

Adam had rushed them off the *Voyager* so fast Cobie's head was still spinning. She grabbed the phone and handed it to Adam. She wanted to hear what he would tell Ray, but then decided to go below deck, stow the bags and make some hot chocolate. Something to chase away the chill and warm up her insides.

She grabbed the bags and made her way through the door and down below deck. After flipping on the lights in the small galley, she set out a couple of mugs. An eerie feeling crawled over her, and Cobie suddenly realized they hadn't even checked the boat. What if the man who'd tried to kill them was on Adam's boat?

Cobie grabbed a large knife, and crept forward, switching on lights in the two small cabins. An odd smell made her crinkle her nose, and she flipped on the light in the stateroom.

A dead body lay sprawled on the bed—Mike Johns, the man who'd warned her to leave.

"Adam!"

Cobie's shriek, the terror in her eyes as she burst into the wheelhouse, had Adam fumbling for traction. He released the wheel and slowed the boat. Gripped her shoulders. "What? What happened, Cobie?"

As she tried to form the words, Adam was keenly aware of their surroundings. Had someone been below deck? In their hurry to leave, they'd failed to look. He realized that now, all these thoughts hitting him at the same moment.

Eyes wide, lips trembling, Cobie said, "A dead man. He's on the bed. It's…it's Mike Johns."

She trembled, and Adam fought the need to comfort her. "Wait here and lock the door behind me."

He grabbed his weapon.

"He's dead, Adam. What are you doing?"

"His killer could still be down there."

When he made it to the steps, he looked at her. Searched the water around them, the islands. They were alone; she'd be safer here than below.

"Stay put. If you see anything suspicious, come and get me. But I won't be long. Understand?"

"Yes. But, Adam, it's the man who warned me."

"Warned you?" He didn't like the sound of that. "Somebody warned you about what?"

"He told me we should leave." Cobie averted her gaze. "You want me to call Ray, tell him the news?"

The sound of another boat in the distance drew Adam's attention. "Yeah, get that call started. I'll be right back after I check everything."

He started down.

"Adam."

He paused. Looked back. "Yeah?"

"Be careful." Something deep and caring shimmered in her big blue eyes.

That goes without saying. But all the same, he liked hearing her say the words. Liked the undercurrent of concern in her tone, even though he knew better than to let it get to him. But maybe it was too late.

He crept down the steps, then checked every corner, every closet. Cobie had been down there; he'd let Cobie go down there by herself. Neither of them had taken any precautions. He'd locked up, yes, and he'd trusted that. And he hadn't unlocked it for her to come down.

Someone had broken in.

And the body on the bed in the stateroom drove that point home. Adam entered the room and glanced inside the bathroom, the shower, the closet. Whoever had left the body was gone already, and he thanked God for that small favor. But why leave the body? Another warning? Was someone unhappy that she'd tried to ask this man questions?

He couldn't believe she hadn't told him about her conversation with the man, but they hadn't had a lot of time to talk. Things had moved quickly after dining with the crew.

He paused in the galley, rubbing his temples. What should they do now, with a dead guy on the boat, besides calling Ray?

"Adam!"

He blew out a breath and bounded up the steps. As soon as he was above deck, he saw a boat getting closer.

"You wanted to know if there was anything suspicious. I've seen that boat several times. Maybe it's nothing, but…"

Adam took a cursory glance at the boat. All he could make out was a guy at the helm. Adam started his boat up again and headed forward. The faster he got them to Mountain Cove, the better. "Yeah, could be nothing. Could be someone needs to reach us, but I'm not taking any chances. Did you get a hold of Ray?"

"I left him a message about the dead guy and that someone tried to kill me so we're headed back to Mountain Cove. I hope that's enough."

That brought a half chuckle. "I'd say that's enough. The boat's gaining on us. Let me try something."

Adam increased speed. The boat behind them sped up, too.

"Can you see who's driving?" he asked. "Is he close enough that you can see his face?"

She shook her head. "I'll get the binoculars. Are you thinking it's the guy who attacked us last night?"

"Could be. And we really need to get Ray on the phone. Tell him someone is after us."

"Okay, which one first?"

"I'll call Ray—you grab the binoculars in my bag."

Adam glanced at the gas gauge, and fear gutted him. What had happened to the gas in his tank? They were going to run out of gas. Maybe the guy chasing them had planned this. Wanted them to run out of gas on the way to their destination. He was one step ahead of them. Adam needed to turn things around and fast.

Cobie appeared. "Got 'em." She held up the binoculars and peered through them.

"If it's him, he's not wearing a mask this time. Have you seen him before?" Adam asked.

"Yes. It's not the captain." That news brought a measure of relief. He hadn't wanted to believe the captain would cause them physical harm, but regardless, he'd certainly put them in harm's way.

"Then where have you seen him? On the *Voyager*?"

"No, in my window that night. And somewhere else, but I can't place it." Her eyes grew wide, could suck him in. "What are we going to do?"

"We're not going to make it to Mountain Cove.

I'm almost out of gas. I think I can get us to Kessler Island. It's going to be close. We might have to drift and hope we have enough momentum to carry us close enough to reach the shore."

"Are you telling me we're going to hide on the same island where this all started?"

"Yeah. Call Ray again, and then Chief Winters. Let them know we're in trouble and where this is going down."

While the boat chugged, sputtering as it used up the last of the fuel, Adam tried the radio, the emergency frequency, attempting to make contact. The Coast Guard could get here quicker. The boat finally burned up the fuel, and he steered toward the island, hoping and praying it would coast them close enough.

They could stay and fight. He had a weapon, after all. But he had limited ammunition. What if Cobie got hurt? Killed? No, their best chance was to hide on the island until the authorities arrived.

The boat drifted closer to shore…closer… The sound of the other boat grew louder as it raced around the island. Too bad there wasn't a way to hide his boat. But the man had seen where they'd gone, so it was pointless.

"Adam, we need to charge the SAT phone. The battery is dead."

And so is the radio.

TWENTY-ONE

The other boat would come around the corner any minute. Whoever the killer was had sabotaged Adam's boat to leave them stranded with no way to call for help.

"No time for that now, Cobie. The boat isn't going much farther. We have to jump in and wade the rest of the way."

"But—"

"Now! There's no time. We have to get a head start in order to lose him and hide." Adam hoped that Ray would get the messages and investigate. Come in search of them when they didn't show up in Mountain Cove. But if Ray didn't understand the urgency, then he might be too late.

Adam jumped into the cold water, which came up to his waist and shocked him to the core. "Here— climb down and then I'll catch you. I can carry you so you don't have to get wet."

Cobie jumped into the water next to him. "No deal. That'll only slow us down."

Hurrying as they waded was like running in one of those dreams where no matter how hard or fast you ran, you couldn't seem to make any headway.

God, please let us make the beach and get out of sight before the other boat arrives. Let me keep her from harm.

Finally they stumbled forward onto the beach and out of the water. The boat carrying the man after them came into the cove, and Adam pulled Cobie into the bushes. "Come on—let's move it. We can stay hidden in the trees, but we have to get away from the beach."

Their pursuer would see their footprints on the beach, anyway, but every minute they could save before he found them counted. Together, they maneuvered through the thick island underbrush, running when they could.

"Where are you taking us?" Cobie gasped for breath.

Adam breathed hard, too. Running up an incline, or trying to, burned his lungs and legs, and having a knife wound to the side didn't help. "To the top. I figured that would give us the advantage."

"Or make us an easy target." Cobie tugged his coat sleeve. "Hold on… Let me catch my breath. Do you think he's onto us?"

Rain started again, splattering the leaves, breaking through the canopy. "If he's not, it won't be long."

He turned and pushed through, putting as much distance as he could between them and the man after them. The guy might have stopped to search the boat, but most likely he was already combing the island and would be on their trail soon. Adam wasn't sure the rain was hard enough to wash their footprints away. Their best chance was to make a beeline for the top. Up there, they couldn't be ambushed. They could watch for him and wait for help to arrive.

In the distance, they saw the cabin. "There's one place we won't be going."

He grabbed her hand and led her away, keeping to the trees, and listening for the man coming for them. They wound their way around the island, not exactly a straight line, but the best way to get to the top. Of course, the man after them might figure out this was Adam's plan, so maybe he should change it up. A waterfall spilled into a crystal clear river that led back out to the ocean, the water bursting from somewhere inside the earth. Maybe it ran through the cave.

Expecting Cobie to follow, he started up, knowing that the hike would be rocky and steep.

"Wait!" Cobie yelled.

He whirled and pressed a finger to his lips. She waited a few yards back. He closed the distance.

"You need to stick with me," he said.

"I need to rest for a few minutes, okay? And you

do, too. I don't want you to overdo it, Adam, or you'll break open your stitches."

Oh, so that's what this was about. She was purposefully trying to slow him down.

"The condition of my stitches won't matter if he finds us."

He frowned and glanced up at the path he'd planned to take. What if the man beat them to it? What if he already had the advantage? He probably traveled much quicker than Adam was moving with Cobie.

"Okay. Change of plans," he said.

"What? Why?" Cobie's eyes were wide, and bluer than ever. Misty droplets rested on her lashes.

This wasn't how he thought things would turn out. Not now. Not before. All he wanted to do was pull her into his arms and… And what? Wish them to another time and place? He couldn't change their shared past. He couldn't change that mistake he'd made. He'd been young and foolish. He realized that this had been more than just him doing what Brad had wanted him to do, protect his sister. This had been about helping her, yes, but trying to somehow undo the wrong he'd done.

"Adam…" She spoke softly now, pulling him from his daze. "What are you thinking about?" She wiped a finger down his cheek. "You're cut. A scrape. Are you feeling okay? Is your side bothering you?"

With her words, he felt the throbbing he'd largely ignored until now. "I'm fine, Cobie, just fine."

But the way her big blue eyes stared up at him, the concern she projected, he knew his heart was anything but fine.

He tugged her close and brought her with him under an outcropping of rock and ferns. Made sure he had a round chambered in his gun in case it came to that. He wasn't sure how things had gotten this out of control. Where had they gone wrong, exactly? Or when someone was trying to kill you, did every choice you made lead you down a harrowing path until it was over?

The waterfall roared at his back, so he pressed his face near her ears, feeling her soft but wet strands against his lips.

"Why is this guy after you? Why does he want to kill you? If he thought you had information he wanted, why would he try to kill you or silence you if he was still searching?"

"He must need to silence me because he thinks I know something. The captain said my father had a secret he took with him when he left the *Voyager.* And he took it with him when he died. It has to be about the Fabergé egg. I thought we already decided that."

"No, *you* decided that. You never told me why. You never even told me who wanted the egg."

"We've been busy trying to stay alive. Trying to leave the *Voyager*. I needed to think on it."

"And now?"

He heard her sharp intake of breath. "I saw the man on the boat in my window, that night, and I also saw his face on Dr. Burkov's phone when I went to meet him for coffee that day. Remember I told you Yuri had something to show me at his house? Something about him that day made me uncomfortable. But maybe he had wanted to show me his collection. He's a private collector."

"What does that mean exactly?"

"He collects artifacts or items of historical significance. Paintings and other valuable pieces. I'm not supposed to know about it, but I overheard my father talking to him once about it when I was a child. I don't think he approved, so perhaps some items weren't acquired legitimately. I don't know. But maybe Yuri wanted me to see it so he could tell me about the egg. Convince me to help him find it."

"And he wanted the egg for his collection why?"

"Does he need a reason?" Cobie pressed a hand to her lips. "It's valuable. Rare. He's Russian, a collector, and perhaps wanted a part of his rich heritage. Somehow he knew that egg was on the ship that went down. He could have been the driving force behind salvaging the wreck, convincing the state and others the gold existed to get them to fall in line. I'm making presumptions here. And maybe…

Maybe the captain really didn't know what someone was after."

Still didn't explain why someone was trying
to kill Cobie, unless they just wanted her to stop
searching for answers to her father's death. She'd
gotten too close, and they needed her out of the
picture.

The cold muzzle of a gun pressed against
Adam's temple.

The man from the boat, the man with the weapon,
directed their path. Cobie knew that Adam had tried
to protect them, and maybe it was her fault for making them stop, for distracting him with her theory,
which meant they'd been caught unawares. And that
waterfall—so beautiful, so enticing—had prevented
either of them from hearing the man's approach.

And now here they were, making their way down
and around, over the rough terrain of the rocky side
of the island until they finally made it to the sea
cave. The other entrance to the cave her father had
written about.

The tide was low now, making it possible to enter
the cave, which they did, stepping over rocks and
pebbles and around boulders. A shiver crawled over
her that had nothing to do with the fact that she was
cold and wet. Was this how they had killed her father? Brought him to this cave to drown?

Adam led the way, and Cobie followed with the

killer at her back, wielding his weapon. When Adam paused and looked behind him, the man barked at him to keep going.

Soon enough, Cobie saw why—another man stood in the shadows, then stepped out, light from the sea cave opening illuminating his face.

"I trusted you," she said. "I didn't believe you were involved in this."

When the captain shrugged, his sad eyes convinced her he was sorry. But what did his sorrow matter?

"I didn't want to be involved. I wanted you to figure out what he needed to know about the egg, so you could go back to your life." A small wave crashed at the entrance as if to emphasize his words. "I didn't know he had tried to kill you. I had nothing to do with that. And that had nothing to do with the egg. I didn't know what he was after when I signed on to this."

The tide was rising.

"Who is trying to kill me besides this guy? What's it all about if not the egg? The gold?"

While the unmasked killer kept his weapon aimed in Cobie and Adam's direction, the captain had his hands stuck in his pocket. Did he also have a weapon?

"The man who raised the funding for much of this operation. At the start we were on contract with the insurance company who paid when the steamer went down. They wanted us to search for gold they had insured. But first we spent years on research and then another five years in a legal battle with another salvage company. With so many obstacles, our potential return on investment plummeted. And then there arose doubts the gold even existed. After a century of searching, of trying to retrieve it, the gold was steeped in mystery. Had almost become a legend." Captain Wainwright paused and glanced behind Cobie.

She followed his gaze to the flashlight waving in the distance. They waited until it drew near.

"Dr. Burkov." The man carrying the light was no surprise to her.

"Hello, my dear. I'm sorry to see things end this way. But since you've searched so hard for an explanation, I believe you deserve one. As the good captain was about to tell you, I was able to work out an agreement. An arrangement with friends in high places—at the insurance company and at the state level—that would allow us to continue the search and retrieval of gold bullion worth millions. Our very special arrangement meant that officially we wouldn't find any gold—why not leave a legend a legend? Makes the history so much more interesting, don't you think? Unofficially, we would receive the lion's share of the market value of the gold."

He glanced behind him and nodded. "Hidden in

this cave for the time being. One of thousands un-discovered on these islands."

"That's why my father was in the cave? He was looking for where you'd hidden the gold?"

"My dear, your father scouted out the cave for us to begin with. A place to store the gold until processing could be arranged. This wouldn't have been the first time he was involved in…let's just say re-distribution of artifacts. But in the end your father wouldn't go along with the arrangement. He said something about a change of heart."

"No, my father was never involved in anything illicit."

Yuri smirked. "How do you think I got my private collection? Your father helped me build it. And I remained his best reference."

No, she wouldn't believe it. Squeezing her eyes shut, she held back a sob. But all Cobie could think about were the vague writings in his journal, the pages that had been ripped out, probably by his own hand. He hadn't wanted anyone to ever know or read the full extent of what he'd done. But in the end, he'd wanted the truth to come out if something happened to him, so he left the journal for Cobie. He knew eventually she would discover the truth.

Searching out that cave, a place to hide the gold, he must have thought of his son who had died in a cave, and maybe his heart had broken for the daughter he'd left behind. That had been enough to change his heart.

And that had led to his demise.

"But this time he wouldn't give me the one thing I wanted. The one thing I've spent my life preparing to retrieve. I handpicked this crew and Deep Water Marine Salvage."

"My daughter." The captain hung his head. "This was the only way to get enough money to pay for her cancer treatments. She has no insurance."

So Dr. Burkov had used Captain Wainwright's misfortune as leverage. She let her gaze settle on him again.

"I had to raise significant funds, work the appropriate channels. I knew if anyone else got their hands on the egg, I might never see it again. Or they would give it or sell it to a museum for the world to see. But the egg belongs in my family. Was given to my great-great-grandmother, who was mistress to Nicholas II. He loved her deeply and so had the egg created as a gift for her. It is still considered one of the lost eggs. When he no longer wished to see her, she took the egg with her, and smuggled it out of Russia long before the revolution or the Romanovs were murdered. My great-uncle Borice Demetriov had the Fabergé egg with him on the SS *Bateman* when it went down. The *Voyager* crew could have their share of the gold. And I could have the egg. In fact, with your father involved, there was no need for them to know of the egg. It was his job to discover it and bring it to me. Then he was killed." Dr. Burkov glared at the man holding the gun.

"And then I interfered," Cobie added.

"Yes, as soon as you showed up on the island, I knew you either knew something or had something of his that could help me find the egg. A journal perhaps? I wanted to find out where he'd hidden the Fabergé egg. But Gustav here—" Dr. Burkov gestured at the armed man "—is a hired assassin and works for Williams, my friend at the insurance company. He was guarding the cave to make sure no one uncovered our stash. And when you appeared, he wanted you dead. You were too close—to the gold and to your father's body—and he didn't know what your father had told you, if you'd come looking for the gold. It was too coincidental that you would show up at the cave. Since Williams could have no part of the egg, he cared nothing about it or finding it."

"But cavers were set to map the cave that day. You had more than me to worry about."

"Complications we would have managed as necessary. Wainwright's crew was set to remove the gold and transport it to a new location, and all we could do was wait and see. Chances are the cavers wouldn't have mapped all the way to the sea cave before leaving and coming back another day."

"But if you needed me alive to find the egg, why try to kill me? Why blow up my business?"

"Again, I wasn't trying to kill you. The bomb wasn't meant to kill anyone. It was set to go off after hours. That was only meant to distract you. After all, you'd have to spend all your time and energy rebuilding, as opposed to searching for why your father died. Williams agreed to this one deviation, but that didn't stop you."

"You forgot. I was also searching for who had tried to kill me. Who was lurking around my house."

"Yes. I persuaded Gustav to search for information about the egg or perhaps find the egg itself, hidden at your home. I became desperate. Mistakes were made, a result of too many fingers in the pie. Initially, Captain Wainwright believed that seeing the *Voyager* would satisfy you. Convince you that your father hadn't been involved in anything underhanded. But then I shared with Wainwright about the egg and that I needed to know what you knew or could find in your father's things. He suspected something all along, but he used you to search where he'd failed. All of this has led us here, to this moment."

Fear gripped Cobie's heart, her whole being sagged under the weight of dread. Dr. Burkov had told them everything. With her eyes she begged both Dr. Burkov and the captain. "What are you going to do with us?"

"I think you know, my dear." He sighed. "So beautiful. Such a waste."

"No! Please, I can find the egg. Adam and I, we'll find the egg for you."

"And then what?" Dr. Burkov shook his head. "You've already spoken with the police. Even if you could use the egg to bargain, I'm afraid I can't trust you. But I'll do what I can to help the police solve the mystery of your disappearance. And then when the case is closed, I'll have time to search for what your father took from me. I've been patient this long."

Anger ignited inside. "If my father kept the egg from you, he had his reasons."

"You didn't know your father very well, as you've admitted, so you can only guess at his reasons. I'll share one more thing about him, so that you can understand him better. The only reason he turned to the black market to begin with was to pay for his wife's survival."

"What are you talking about?"

"She had ovarian cancer while she was pregnant with you."

"No, that can't be true. She died giving birth to me."

"A few months after, the cancer had gone too far. He used the black market money to buy the best medicine had to offer, and still it wasn't enough to save her. I'm sorry to tell you this now, as you face your own death, but you deserve to know. Still, I think you must have been the motivation behind his attempt to right his wrongs in the end. To change the course of his life. But he picked the wrong time to do it, the wrong person to turn his back on."

Adam lunged for Gustav, the hired assassin.

But Gustav only grabbed Cobie and pressed the gun in her temple.

"Why don't you just shoot me now and get it over with?"

"The time of death has to be right." Dr. Burkov spoke to Gustav now as much as to Cobie and Adam. "We don't want this to look like a murder. A gunshot wound would bring more questions. We're removing the rest of the gold today, so there won't be anything to find but your bodies. To the authorities it will look like you and Adam were exploring the cave after leaving the *Voyager*, looking for answers again, when you were caught up in the flooding. So much more appropriate, don't you think?"

That was how her brother had died and then her father, too. Tears burned her eyes. "You're a monster."

"No, I'm a historian. And history repeats itself."

TWENTY-TWO

No way.

No way would Adam let this go any further. He might as well die trying. When Gustav handed his weapon over to Dr. Burkov so he could tie Adam's wrists, Adam dived for the guy's midsection and plowed into him, shoving him into boulders. For that, Adam earned a smash in the head. A kick in his wound. Dazed into a half-conscious state, he couldn't move. Seawater slapped at him, washed over him and burned the now-seeping knife wound.

Then he felt himself being hefted and dragged. Before he could shake off his stupor and the pain or snatch his hands away, his wrists were tied in a serious knot, the marine rope linked through a rusty iron loop secured in the rock. He was helpless, worthless to save her. How could it be that they would both die this way?

Gustav reached for Cobie, but she stepped over to Dr. Burkov and slapped him across the face. "You were one of my father's closest friends. How could you do that? How could you kill him? How could you do this to me, his daughter?"

His eyes flashed. "I tried to talk to you that day. Had planned to show you everything. Reason with you. I could tell that all you wanted were answers. I...thought I could trust you with information about the egg. But when you ran from me, I knew I couldn't."

"But how will you find it? If my father knew something... Please."

He said nothing, just shook his head. "I'm sorry."

Gustav grabbed her. Carried her screaming and kicking. "If you don't cooperate, I'll have to knock you unconscious, and you won't have these last few precious moments of your life to say your goodbyes."

Adam watched as Cobie sagged against Gustav, all the fight rushing out of her. He watched as Gustav secured Cobie's wrists, tying a complicated and secure knot. He and Cobie couldn't get out of this.

Not without help from above.

"The tide's rising. We'll have to wait to remove the gold," Wainwright finally spoke up. "But once they're...gone...we'll free them to wash farther into the cave with the next tide, just as we did with her father."

"Should have let me get rid of them," Gustav said. "Then we'd be done."

"That would be too harsh, too brutal," Yuri replied. "This is more poetic."

"Poetic?" Adam yelled at the top of his lungs. "Is that your answer to this?"

The men left them, taking the light with them. Once Adam's eyes adjusted to the dark, the dim light from the entrance allowed him to see the outline of Cobie's form next to him. Her face. He didn't need to see her to know she was terrified at what was to come. Her ragged breaths, bordering on hyperventilation, told him enough. And if not for her breaths, he'd know anyway—he was experiencing the same terror.

The waves splashed, spilling over the rocks and rushing toward them, soaking their shoes and pants. Adam thought Gustav's way—to end things quickly—might have been more merciful. Instead they had been left to suffer in terror until the ocean finally took them.

Adam squeezed his eyes shut, the pain of memories crashing over him. Both he and Brad had played a deadly game, going into the cave that they knew would flood.

Played a game and lost.

Should he tell Cobie how sorry he was, one last time? Would she want to hear it now?

"I'm sorry, Cobie. So sorry about your brother. I can never take it back, but if I could…"

"Tell me." A raspy desperation filled her voice. "I

want to hear the life you dreamed about if Brad had lived. If Brad hadn't died and changed everything."

Her words surprised him. He wasn't sure what to say. How to answer her. But hadn't he dreamed about how life would have been different a thousand times? The ocean rolled up and over them now, covering his legs.

He'd better hurry. Panic was starting to get to him. *My grandmother, my family...this will devastate them.*

"Adam, tell me now. I need to know what might have been."

What might have been... *Oh, God, I want to live. I want the chance to have a future, in spite of the past!*

Adam tried to pull his hand out of the rope, but Gustav knew what he was doing and there was no way to get free. Cobie was tied closer to the water than Adam was. Why? Why had they done that?

He wouldn't stop tugging; he'd keep at it until he died or escaped. One or the other. "Cobie, I'll tell you, but first I want you to try to squeeze your hand through the rope."

He wondered if it would be possible for them to actually break their own hands to free themselves, but then how would they climb out of there, swim out?

The water came in faster, and Adam glanced at Cobie. She would be under before he would. She would drown first. And his heart stumbled over the futility of it all. He should have let himself love her while he had the chance. He should have told her. She started sobbing, spitting water. She stood, but the rope kept her close to the ground, pulled her head down.

"Adam, please. I don't have much longer."

"If Brad hadn't drowned that day. If I hadn't been the reason, or blamed myself, and if that hadn't stood between us, then I think, eventually, I would have told you."

A big wave rolled up and over them.

"Told me what, Adam?" Cobie coughed.

"That I loved you, Cobie!" A sob cracked Adam's voice. "That I love you. Brad didn't think I was good enough for you, so I could never tell you, but my feelings for you never stopped, never went away. So if he hadn't died, if you hadn't hated me, then eventually I would have told you anyway. Even though he was my best friend."

There, he'd said it, but it didn't matter. The ocean wouldn't stop rushing in on them. The moon wouldn't stop its pull from the opposite side of the world just because Adam told Cobie that he'd always loved her.

Cold salt water washed over her, making her numb, so numb. Just like when she'd jumped into the water to escape a killer. She should have died then, before getting Adam involved. He'd die today because of her.

She might have less than five minutes before the ocean took her this time.

But Adam had just told her that he loved her. And Cobie didn't know what to do with that. It was everything she'd dreamed about before Brad's death. Before her world had been destroyed. And, yeah, she'd blamed Adam. But even if she hadn't blamed him, she'd still mentally connected him with Brad. Looking at him had just made her relive her loss and the pain it caused her. But somewhere along the line, that had changed. And now, before she died, she had to do it. She had to forgive him.

God, help me to do it. To really forgive him all the way, deep in my heart. I know I can't die without doing this. The water level was so high now that Cobie had to twist around and raise her face to the side to breathe.

"Adam, listen up."

Water moved in and around her mouth and into her nose. *God, please, no! Not yet!* She coughed, spat the ocean out. *Let me tell him...please...*

"I forgive you, Adam. I don't hold you responsible anymore. It wasn't your fault. Brad had a choice. You both made mistakes. But even if it was all your fault—" Cobie wasn't sure she could finish after another crashing wave "—I forgive you."

Cobie couldn't know if Adam heard her, except

she thought she heard him shouting something. The cold ocean swirled around her head and face, as she held her breath, squeezed her eyes shut. She couldn't hold it much longer, but survival was built into human DNA. She would hold on to that last breath of life as long as she could.

She saw a light in the distance. Was that the light people always talked about seeing when they died? Those who'd been revived? She didn't think she was dead yet. Her lungs were screaming. No. She was very much alive.

But not for much longer.

The light…

It grew closer.

"Adam…" The word gurgled out with the last of her breath.

Cobie gulped water into her lungs.

"Not me! Save Cobie. Save Cobie!" Adam fought against the rope, nearly ripping his arms out of their sockets to get free. If only he could reach her. Hold her up.

But the water was too deep now, and it covered her head. Was she holding her breath?

He'd yelled at her. Told her to hold her breath a little longer. Someone was coming. Had appeared from the back of the cave entrance, wading in his boots, wearing a headlamp and carrying a separate flashlight. Had to be Ray.

Water rolled over Adam's face now. He knew they had hope, so he held his breath. Ray would get them out. He'd obviously gotten their messages and come in search of them. Seen Adam's boat.

He hoped Ray would hurry because he couldn't hold his breath much longer. Ray shook his shoulder, and then suddenly Adam was free. He lifted his head from the water, sucked in breath. He was free, and his first thought was for Cobie.

Wainwright held her. Adam looked around him. Ray wasn't there.

"Wainwright?" Adam took Cobie from him.

"Come on—let's get out of here, get her somewhere where we can perform CPR." Wainwright led the way.

Stumbling after him, Adam wasn't sure what he would do, how he would go on, if Cobie died. But she'd gone under mere seconds before Adam had seen the flashlight from the back of the cave. Surely it wasn't too late.

Wainwright ran ahead of him and climbed through the cave to a higher elevation, crouching as he went. Adam followed. The man appeared to know the way, and he'd come back for them. Adam didn't know what to think about that. He'd wanted to kill the captain earlier. Adam's body was numb and cold, and his legs shook at the sight of Cobie lying so still.

"The water's cold, very cold, which is a plus for

her." Wainwright stopped. "You can put her here on the sand. Give her CPR."

Adam leaned over her; then she sputtered, coughed and rolled to her side.

Adam gathered her into his arms. They could warm each other up this way. "Cobie... I thought I'd lost you forever."

He held her tightly, weaved his fingers into her wet hair.

"Adam, I know you need a moment, but—"

"I saw a light," Cobie said, choking on a sob. "I saw light, and all I could think about, could wonder, is if that was what Brad saw when he died. You know how they say people see the light, follow the light when they die? I know that Jesus is the light, and Brad knew Him, he knew his savior. That's been my one consolation through it all. But...when I saw the light, I wondered if I was dying. Then everything went black."

Adam held her tighter, and they both sobbed in each other's arms. So grateful for life. So grateful to be alive. "Cobie, Wainwright came back. He cut the ropes. He saved us."

When Adam relinquished his hold, she looked shocked and turned to Wainwright.

"Thank you," she said.

"Listen," Wainwright said. "This leg of the cave is going to be underwater in a matter of minutes. Let's get out of here."

Adam wasn't sure, but he might never go in a cave again. Wainwright led the way, followed by Cobie and then Adam. It must be raining hard outside, the way the water trickled through the limestone and washed over the sides. Adam was glad that Wainwright knew his way out or else they could still get stuck and drown. "Does this lead to the river?"

"Sure does. That's why we have to hurry. Stay close. I only have this one flashlight."

Water spilled over the cave floor like a small brook. In front of him, Cobie slipped down.

"Hold up."

She righted herself, but Adam knew they were both running on fear-induced adrenaline. "Thanks, I'm okay. Let's go."

They continued on; then Wainwright slowed. "This part gets tricky. It's a narrow tube, goes on for a few feet. We'll need to hurry before it fills completely with water. Then we'll be home free." He held the light up, looking into their faces. "Understand?"

Cobie's eyes were wild. She'd just experienced what it felt like to drown. "Hurry. Let's do it." The panic in her tone held the same urgency that Adam felt.

Wainwright dropped down into the flow of water and started crawling forward. The light would soon disappear with him. "Go on, Cobie—stay with him.

I'll be right behind you. Stay with him. Stay with the light."

They made it through the tube and clung to the holes in the slippery cave walls where the river began to swell. Adam knew this was how her father had ended up washed into the upper part of the cave. They would climb their way there now, but it was a race against the flooding waters. A race against time.

Adam had been through this experience before, and someone had died then.

God, if anyone has to die this time, please let it be me. Save Cobie. Let her live.

As the water rose faster than Adam ever could have imagined, he feared that none of them would make it out in time.

TWENTY-THREE

Cobie followed the light, the same light she'd seen just before she drowned. She followed the captain, trying to escape the water pouring from every nook and hole in the cave.

She was still unable to comprehend that he'd come back for them. When his flashlight flickered, sheer panic had her leaning against the cool limestone wall. The captain smacked the flashlight a couple of times, and it flickered brighter. But how long could that last? At least he had his headlamp. But if that went? Without light, they would never find their way out.

"We're climbing now, and water is running down, so be careful," he said.

He was right. Cobie could hardly grip the slick surface. If she slipped, started sliding back, she'd take Adam with her. With everything in her, she dug into the rock and sand, grunting and willing her way up. The water rushed beneath her to meet the rising water below. Eventually it would fill this entire cavern.

"How much farther?" Adam called from behind.

"Almost there. I promise."

Cobie wanted to know why he'd come back. Why the change of heart. But she'd ask about that later. She had a feeling she knew. He'd never signed on for murder to begin with. He hadn't wanted any part of killing someone, much less killing a friend. And she still believed that her father had been his friend. In his own way, the captain had tried to protect them, but he had Gustav to deal with and Dr. Burkov.

It was all too much to think about as her energy waned. Exhaustion spread through every limb. This felt like a living nightmare—crawling through the waning light, darkness coming after her, the real threat of water cutting her off from escape.

She couldn't go through drowning again. The sheer panic and terror of knowing it was coming, holding her breath as long as she could until her body betrayed her.

Someone caught her arm, yanked her free from the terrifying thoughts and pulled her up. The captain assisted Adam up behind her. "We're almost there. I think the water washes debris and—"

He cut himself off before he could add the word *bodies*. Cobie let out a sharp breath. "Now what?"

A light flicked on. *Gustav.* "Now it's time to end this for real."

"No, Gustav, this has to stop," the captain ordered.

Gustav fired his weapon, and the captain fell back. Cobie screamed and dived out of the way as Adam rammed into Gustav, wrestling with him for the gun. Cobie had to help. The flashlight lay on the ground, illuminating the cavern.

Adam slammed Gustav's wrist against the ground repeatedly as grunts and groans escaped both men.

What should I do? What can I do? God, show me...

The gun slid across the cave floor. This part of the cave had not yet flooded. Cobie stumbled to the weapon and wrapped her hand around the grip. Hands shaking—far too much to risk shooting—she aimed nonetheless.

"Stop it. I have the gun now. So stop it."

Neither man listened to her, just kept pounding each other. If Cobie could have, she would have joined Adam in punching him. She wanted to hurt this murderer, this hired assassin, the man who'd tried to kill her. The same man who had tied her father down in the sea cave to drown him, murdering him. The man who had just shot Captain Wainwright.

Aiming the gun away, she fired the weapon. Pain sliced through her ears, left them ringing.

But that had done the trick. Both men stopped fighting. Adam had wanted to get the upper hand, she knew, but she couldn't risk Gustav killing him. Both men stood motionless, watching Cobie.

"Careful now, Cobie. I'm coming toward you." Adam started forward.

She imagined her trembling hands made him nervous. They made her nervous, too. But she had no intention of letting this man kill another person. Before she could think or react, Gustav jabbed a knife against Adam's throat.

It drew blood. Even from here, in the dim flicker of the flashlight, Cobie could see that he meant business. She wanted to shoot him, to kill him now, but she wasn't a marksman and could just as likely kill Adam.

Gustav laughed at her, a taunting laugh. "If it had been up to me, I would have killed you in the sea cave. I'm not big on poetry. I would have killed you at the cave entrance if you hadn't hit me. So I owe you for that."

Cobie had to keep him talking, keep Adam alive for as long as he could. She shared a look with him and replayed the words he'd said to her just before the water had crashed over her. She wanted to live again, she wanted a life with him, and she wasn't going to let this maniac take that from her. "You killed my father."

He twisted the knife so it glinted in the light. "He drowned."

"Because you tied him down in the sea cave."

"Wasn't my idea, but we have to make things look like an accident. Dr. Burkov says you have a family history of it."

That's it. Cobie aimed, pressed her finger against the trigger. *Oh, God, please help me. Adam, please...please move away...*

Gunfire rang out, echoing through the cave. Adam shoved away from Gustav, who slumped to the ground.

Adam jerked his gaze to Cobie. "Oh..." The breath rushed from her. She dropped the gun. "It wasn't me. I didn't shoot."

Adam glanced behind him.

Pressing a hand to his side, Wainwright stumbled forward. "Lucky for you, he didn't kill me."

Careful of his injury, Adam grabbed Wainwright in a bear hug, which seemed kind of weird, considering, but emotions ran high. The man had saved them, twice. Then Adam glanced over to where Cobie looked as if she would collapse, but she composed herself and came over to Adam.

"I don't know, Wainwright. I think Cobie was about to shoot." He'd seen that wild look in her eyes and had tensed up, prepared to duck away, at great risk to his life and limb. But it was either the knife or a gunshot wound.

Adam grabbed Cobie to him. "Let's get out of

here before anyone else shows up. Wainwright, you okay to walk?"

"I'm good for now."

Adam leaned down, checked Gustav's pulse. "He's dead." He lifted the body in a fireman's carry, keenly feeling the pain in his side. No matter how bad the man, he didn't think anyone should be left unburied, as Cobie's father had been. He would get his burial soon enough. They knew how he had died now.

Following Wainwright and Cobie, Adam carried Gustav until they made the crawlway entrance, where they all had to slide through. Adam and Wainwright maneuvered Gustav's body through the hole.

When Adam crawled out of the cave, he saw they'd been met by law enforcement at the entrance. Coast Guard and Forest Service LEIs and a couple of Alaska state troopers. Ray stood there, as well; he'd obviously called in the troops.

"Looks like I'm too late," he said. "So tell me what's happened."

Adam explained what he could and then left Wainwright to tell his story to Ray and the state troopers. By saving them, the man had given himself up, given it all up.

When Ray approached, Adam asked, "How did you know to come here? To call in the cavalry?"

"I got your messages. Then when I saw your boat,

I also saw their boats just out a ways from the sea cave, and I put two and two together. They must have spotted my approach and suspected someone would try to save you and then the truth would come out if you were found alive. That's probably why Gustav came back to wait for your escape. He just didn't know that the long arm of the law had arrived—even out here on an island in the middle of Nowhere, Alaska—and he couldn't escape. Don't worry, Adam. Everyone involved, including Dr. Burkov, will be brought to justice."

A knot grew in Adam's throat. "I'll be forever in your debt."

"But it wasn't me who saved you."

"You couldn't have made it in time, but I know you did everything you could. In an odd twist, Cobie and I owe Captain Wainwright for our lives. He risked everything to save us."

"That he did. It's a tangled web, to be sure, but right now, I think there's someone else you want to talk to."

Adam had already taken his eyes from his friend and was staring at Cobie. A female officer wrapped her in a blanket, covering her head, too. Checking her out to make sure she was okay.

Cobie's gaze flicked to him, and he caught it, held it. Adam squeezed Ray's shoulder and made his way to Cobie.

She came right into his arms, leaving him wondering—again—which of them had made the move, but it didn't matter anymore. Nothing mattered anymore except that she was in his arms. And it was over. It was all over.

The rain poured, but Adam didn't care. He leaned down and pressed his lips to Cobie's—answering a lifetime of dreams about this woman, the woman of his dreams. He hadn't been able to love anyone but her, and after life's tragic turn, he hadn't been able to love *even* her, but now he was willing to risk his heart completely.

And he knew… He knew that moment just before she went under and drowned. He knew because those were her last words to him before she thought she would die—that she had forgiven him. He couldn't have asked for better words.

Well, except there were three words he'd told her, but he knew what it had cost her to tell him she'd let his part in her brother's death go.

And he deepened the kiss, feeling free from the burden that had weighed on him, kept them apart. He knew they were meant to be together, always meant to be together, and Brad, if he watched them now, would give his blessing.

Someone cleared his throat, and though he didn't want to end this moment—their first kiss—especially after a lifetime of dreaming about it, Adam eased back. He'd never forget that look in Cobie's eyes. Maybe she hadn't told him she loved him in so many words, but he saw it in her eyes well enough. Felt it in the way she responded to his kiss.

And that was all he needed to know. He'd meant to travel the world. Gain some perspective on his life, after the tragedy had eaten away at it, and after his business had burned.

He'd found perspective all right. And he had a change of plans. Smiling down at her, he took her hand and led her down the path and back to the beach, where they could get a ride off this island. He knew he had a dreamy look on his face, and that was because he was dreaming about a future with Cobie.

He wouldn't travel the world right now. No, for the next few months he had to work on building a relationship with Cobie MacBride. Making up for all that lost time. He had a purpose and a mission. His siblings… Adam laughed to himself. His siblings had nothing on him.

And yeah. Sure. He'd be home for Christmas.

Christmas this year would be the best one yet. That was, if Cobie went along with his plans.

TWENTY-FOUR

Mountain Cove
Christmas Eve

Three months later, Cobie stood in the dining room in her small home, adjusting the place settings for a Christmas Eve dinner with the Warren siblings, including their families and children. She'd taken a bold step in asking Adam's entire family over. But she wanted the sounds of family and love to fill her home—a house that had seemed lonely, devoid of life and love, for far too long. Though she looked forward to it, she was also nervous. Felt a little awkward. After all, everyone knew how she'd felt about Adam after her brother's death. She'd made that very clear.

But they hadn't known how insanely jealous she'd been of Adam's family. Good thing she'd put that all behind her, including her resentment. Facing death had a way of making a person rethink everything. And God had given her a second chance. A chance to live the life she wanted in more ways than she could count.

She wished things had turned out differently for her father, but she was glad she'd found the closure she'd needed. It still didn't sit well to know her father had been involved in the illicit antiquities market, but at least she was able to understand his reasons, even if she didn't agree with them. He'd certainly paid a high enough price for his crimes. Meanwhile, Captain Wainwright, his crew and Dr. Burkov had been arrested, and the judicial process had started.

The Dancing Stallion Fabergé egg was the only missing piece, and Cobie doubted she would ever know what her father had done with it, or if he had hidden it at all. To tell the truth, she didn't much care. In Adam's love, and in the acceptance from his family, she'd found a treasure that suited her much better.

Hands slid around her waist from behind. Strong, familiar hands. A warm tingle swept over her. Cobie twisted around and pressed into Adam, who quickly planted his lips on hers. More tingles, and that floating sensation she couldn't get enough of.

"I love you," he whispered.

Cobie would never get over the sound of those words in her ears. It was as if he whispered them directly to her heart.

"I love you, too." Cobie ran her hands up and

around his neck and gazed into his eyes. Being in love… There wasn't anything like it.

If she hadn't been willing to let God change her heart, let her forgive, she wouldn't be there right now, standing with a man she loved and being with his big family. She wouldn't have been able to start a new chapter in her life with the man she'd once dreamed about. Adam wouldn't be rebuilding his bike shop right next to where she was rebuilding her dental office.

The way he smiled down at her—as if he had a secret—tripped her heart. "What?"

"I have… I need… Come with me." He released her waist and took her hand, dragging her through the house.

He didn't even stop when the doorbell rang—probably more family—but dragged her through the foyer and to the Christmas tree in the small living room that now contained plenty of new furniture.

"Adam? Cobie?" Leah stood there, holding little Scotty and watching them. "There's a package for you, Cobie."

She gasped, pressed a hand to her throat. "For me?"

She rushed to the door and signed for the package from the courier.

Both excitement and dread coursed through her. "I wonder who it could be from."

She brought the box back into the room as the rest

of the family joined her and Adam. They pressed in, making the room seem much smaller. She'd wanted a big family, but now she was overwhelmed.

"Well, open it," Heidi said.

They all watched her. Weren't they going to give her some privacy?

Cobie frowned but shoved away her irritation. If she was going to be part of this family—and she had an inkling things were leading that way—she'd better get used to it. She'd wanted it, after all.

"Here." Cade handed over a knife. "You can cut open the box quicker that way."

And Cobie did just that. Inside the bubble-wrapped filled box, was another box, an intricately carved, beautiful box. Cobie wasn't sure if the box was the gift itself, but, no, that couldn't be right. It was too heavy to be just an empty case. Something was inside the box.

Who would send her this? Cobie's heart skipped and tumbled as her imagination went wild with possibilities.

She looked at Adam.

"It's not from me," he said, as though reading her mind. And she thought she caught the hint of disappointment in his eyes. What was that about?

Cobie opened the box and nearly dropped the contents.

"Oh…my… It's the…" She couldn't find the words. She turned it for all to see. "It's the Dancing Stallion, one of the imperial Fabergé eggs." If this had come from her father, if it was the one he'd found while salvaging the shipwreck, he had obviously taken the time to have it restored to its original beauty.

Everyone stared at the intricate work of gold and jewels that left them all speechless. Cobie was almost afraid to hold something of this value, especially considering that people had died for this. Her father. Mike Johns. Gustav.

"And...there's more." She was scared to open it. "On the inside should be a surprise. Fabergé created the eggs with surprises."

She flipped open the top to reveal a beautiful stallion, dancing, just as the name implied.

"Cobie, here, look at this. It fell out." Adam handed her an envelope.

From my father. In front of Adam's family, Cobie silently read the very private letter her father had written, telling her that she'd know what to do with the egg. It belonged in a museum. And that if she'd received the letter and the egg, that meant he was dead. That he'd wanted to make up his mistakes to her, was trying to change so many things to make that happen—things that were proving to be too much to overcome. But he told her to never let anything get in the way of loving someone.

Tears slipped freely down her cheeks.

"Well?" Heidi said. "What does it say?"

Cobie laughed through the tears, pressing the letter against her heart. There would be no secrets in this family. "It says that he loves me. That he loved me. That I should make sure the egg goes to a museum. That the world should know a lost egg has been found."

And she knew what that meant... She'd been lost, and now she was found.

Little Scotty chose that moment to burp. Then everyone started talking, bubbling with joy, gathering around her, looking at the egg. And through the chaos, Cobie found Adam, standing back from his family.

She left the egg and went to his side, rose up on her toes and kissed him. Her father had been right. She'd been foolish to let anything get in the way of loving this man.

Adam cleared his throat. "Um...excuse me... Family of mine?"

Everyone stopped and stared.

His face reddened. Cobie had never seen anything so cute, and it made her heart flutter erratically.

"I had planned to do this in private. Just me and Cobie. Was on my way, but my plans have been run aground by a century-old golden egg. But I have gold and jewels of my own to offer. Cobie." He turned his attention to her and dropped to one knee. "Cobie MacBride, will you marry me?"

More tears now, and she swiped at them. Hated to

let them fall with everyone looking on. "Oh, Adam, yes, I'll marry you. I love you. And did you mention more gold and jewels?"

He grinned and pulled out a small black velvet box. Popped it open.

A solitaire diamond straddled by sapphires sparkled in the light. "Oh, Adam, it's beautiful."

"I wanted something to match your beautiful blue eyes."

Cobie tugged him to his feet and let him slip the ring on her finger. "And it's far more beautiful to me than any old Fabergé egg."

* * * * *

Dear Reader,

I hope you enjoyed reading *Submerged* as much as I enjoyed writing it and researching the historical information. Shipwrecks have always fascinated me. We often associate shipwrecks with the Spanish galleons off the coast of Florida. When I learned that three thousand shipwrecks are suspected to rest off the coast of Alaska, I was astounded. Then I read about the SS *Islander*, a steamer traveling from Skagway purported to carry wealthy passengers along with gold bullion in the millions. The SS *Islander* sank in the Inside Passage in 1901, killing forty passengers. There have been several failed salvage attempts over the past century until the gold bullion has almost become a legend. As of this writing, my research indicates that in 2012 a salvage company was granted permission for yet another attempt to salvage the gold, and that is still in process. I created a fictional shipwreck but based my story off the real history of the SS *Islander* shipwreck.

During my research, I also came across the story of a scrap metal entrepreneur who bought a golden egg believing he could melt it down and make a profit on the gold. Turned out that egg was one of the eight lost imperial Fabergé Easter eggs! That got me to thinking how much more fun it would be to include a lost egg in the treasure. Gold is one thing. Even expected. But a Fabergé egg is much better. Again, I created a fictional egg for the story. What if I used a real lost egg in the story and later someone found it?

Along with the history, of course, this fourth installment in the Mountain Cove series had to lean heavily on the stunning setting of southeast Alaska. My characters, who loved to explore caves, called spelunking or caving, experienced a tragedy. In *Submerged*, they return to a cave and face their greatest fears and worst memories and find danger and mystery inside the cave that has them running from a killer in search of the truth.

My heroine, Cobie MacBride, has another kind of mystery to solve. Another kind of treasure to find, and that's forgiveness. If she can somehow forgive Adam for the part he played in her brother's death, she can find freedom from resentment and bitterness, and she can have the treasure of love. Adam must forgive himself, too, and if only Cobie could forgive him, then he would be free of that burden, as well. We don't want to sink to the depth of the ocean, burdened or weighted down because we carry bitterness and resentments, no matter how we believe we've been wronged.

I hope you enjoyed the ride and came away with a spiritual nugget or treasure of your own. I love to connect with my readers, so please drop me a line via my contact page on my website or connect with me through Facebook or Twitter, also found on my website. If you'd like to receive book news and updates, sign up for my newsletter. All this can be found at my website: elizabethgoddard.com.

Many blessings,

Elizabeth Goddard

LARGER-PRINT BOOKS!

GET 2 FREE
LARGER-PRINT NOVELS
PLUS 2 FREE
MYSTERY GIFTS

Love Inspired.
SUSPENSE
RIVETING INSPIRATIONAL ROMANCE

Larger-print novels are now available...

LISLP15

LARGER-PRINT BOOKS!

GET 2 FREE
LARGER-PRINT NOVELS
PLUS 2 FREE
MYSTERY GIFTS

Love Inspired®

Larger-print novels are now available...

LILP15

READERSERVICE.COM

Manage your account online!

- Review your order history
- Manage your payments
- Update your address

> **We've designed the
> Reader Service website
> just for you.**

Enjoy all the features!

- Discover new series available to you, and read excerpts from any series.
- Respond to mailings and special monthly offers.
- Connect with favorite authors at the blog.
- Browse the Bonus Bucks catalog and online-only exculsives.
- Share your feedback.

Visit us at:
ReaderService.com